PLAYED

A BRITISH BAD BOY ROMANCE

International Bestselling Author

NIKKI WILD

Copyright 2015 Nikki Wild

All Rights Reserved

Find me at my website:

WWW.WILDNIKKI.COM

Or friend me on Facebook!

http://www.facebook.com/wildnikki

Table of Contents

Author's Note

Prologue

Lex

My name is Alexander Lambert, but you can call me Lex… after all, everyone else in Great Britain does. My rabid fans, the sportscasters, and the tabloids know me by a slightly different name: "Lightning Lex Lambert."

You see, I'm kind of a big fucking deal.

For the last twelve years, I've been rising in the football world – or *soccer,* as the Americans call it, rather *incorrectly* I'll quickly add.

I've paid my dues, playing in some of the most prestigious teams to grace the great echelons of English football might: some junior teams, Manchester United, Galaxy League, a few seasons here and there with an underdog or two… and now the National team.

Which means one thing:

I'm a *World Cup* caliber player.

The greatest sport on Earth, watched with borderline zealotry by over a hundred countries, all culminating in a grand championship that draws audiences over hundreds of millions. The sheer marketing dollars spent on that tournament outperforms the gross domestic product of smaller countries, *every single year*, and it's only getting bigger and bigger.

And right there on the field?

Me.

Lex Fucking Lambert, star player and team captain of the English National Team. I am the best of the best, a regular household name in my home country. My signature alone is a prized commodity in the realm of sports merchandising. Signed headshots fetch for thousands of dollars on eBay, especially since I've only signed maybe twenty or thirty of them in my entire life.

My reputation for fearless, combative ball is legendary among discussions of the sport. When I step out under the lights and look down my hardened, take-no-prisoners enemies on the field, they *quake* with fear.

I'm known *off* the field as well, although *that* preceding reputation is slightly different… and even more fun.

Let's just say that playing it *family friendly* is a damned good waste of ridiculous fame, staggeringly impeccable physique, and my particular breed of effortlessly rugged features…

I might have been caught in the tabloids a few times with some hot, nameless piece of ass. Or, you know, maybe a lot more than a few.

What can I say? I'm a handsome piece, and I know how to wear a tailored suit… and as it turns out, the women go *crazy* for that kind of thing.

They *all* fancy a shag with Lex.

I had it all – the looks, the game, the prestige, and the effortless, thirsty pussy *thrown* at me every time I walked into a bar. Life was great, and the sex on demand was even better. But I lacked one thing, and I knew *exactly* what it was.

The *big* money.

You might have never heard of the Patrovo Corporation, but they're a bigger deal in Jolly Ole England than *me*.

Hard to imagine, I'm sure.

Pretty much everything from top-tier, high-end sneakers to household boxes of oat cereal are owned by some subsidiary company that eventually bows to the Patrovo Corporation, no matter how high up the food chain you have to go. They have their grubby little fingers in goddamn *everything*… and they dish out one multi-million dollar corporate sponsorships to one lucky star athlete per year… the best of the best.

In case you'd forgotten… that's me.

I *wanted* that contract with every fiber of my being. I burned for it. Nobody else deserved it more than me. I was already a pop culture celebrity, known and beloved by the entire country… and I had the *skills* to back it up.

That money belonged to me.

Which made this little conversation all the more upsetting…

"You do realize *why* you're not getting the sponsorship, yeah?" Jess casually asked as she sipped from her frothing pint of dark ale.

She and I were sitting across from each other at a small, private bar-top table in my favourite pub, *The Grinning Twig*. It was one of the few watering holes that held my authority in such reverence that I could sneak through the back and sit in a private room with a lips-sealed, *mum's the word* bartender.

Jess continued, setting her glass down and wiping the froth from her lips with the back of her hand. "I mean, even *you* aren't that dull in the head, Lex. Surely, you've figured it out by now."

"Go ahead, then," I growled in slight protest; I set my own glass down against the bar with a clatter that rang a little too loudly. My private bartender glanced up from wiping out the mug in his hands, but when it was clear that I didn't give a rat's *arse* about him, he soon resumed his work.

One look at Jess's face, and my mind quickly changed. "Wait, no. You're doing that sodding smirk of yours. Don't do the smirk."

"What smirk?" She asked innocently, her eyes flashing wild with mischievousness. "Couldn't *possibly* know what you're talking about…"

"You're doing it right now," I repeated, my voice gravelly with mounting frustration. "I *know* that smirk. That's the smirk you give that rambunctious, shit-assed pup of yours when he's misbehaving."

Of course, I wasn't referring to a dog. Jess didn't own a dog. What she *did* own was a taste for men barely old enough to move out of their mummy's house… this month, he was a sniveling, spineless punk wannabe.

Kept on a leash like any good dog, Timothy was a scrawny little fuck… a wet-behind-the-ears kid just tall enough to pull off a leather jacket. Even *that* took a little convincing.

Ignoring my criticism of her fuck-buddy choices, Jess's smirk widened, and she reclined against the bar stool, crossing her arms.

"You *know* what I'm going to say."

"Let's pretend that I don't," I insisted.

I didn't like being toyed with, and she knew that. The two people I needed to confide in at times like this were my best friend, and my publicist.

Life put both in the same fucking woman.

What a lucky sod that made me.

Jess watched me for a moment, choosing her words and judging my reactions before finally cutting loose. "Lex, the Patrovo Corporation invests a lot of money into proper *brand* representation. The athletes they slap on the boxes of cereal, or put in their stupid shoe commercials, they need those athletes to protect their interests."

"I'm well aware," I gruffly reminded her.

Jess raised an eyebrow. "I understand that. But what you've got to realize is that Brett Barker plays it safe as shit. His choice is going to be careful, calculated, and *definitely* not you."

"I'm safe," I protested, lifting my arms in dismay before clasping the fingers behind my head. "Safe as they come."

"*Safe* doesn't get their photos slapped across a six-page major spread," she grumbled, reaching into her purse to whip out a creased tabloid. She shoved it towards me, and I lazily leaned back forwards and rifled through the pages.

Sure, I was on the cover again. No big deal.

"I don't see what you're–"

Then I stopped, glancing at the photos. Seemed like the paparazzi fucks had stalked me to a hotel balcony, where I'd been photographed with my arms around two lovely little ladies.

I remembered them. Not their names, of course, but I recalled the three nights of glorious, hardcore lovemaking we'd had together… and how jealous the gods must have been in their various pantheons.

Of course, that didn't matter now.

Not when I was staring at various blurry pictures, showing under no arguable terms that I was kissing one with another on her knees in front of me at cock level. In another candid photo, they were kissing for my entertainment… and in *yet another*, they were *both* at cock level in front of me, with my proud face held high and each palm resting on their heads...

Yeah, I'd almost forgotten how good those few days had been. *Cor blimey,* were they voracious in the hotel bed... and in the shower… and on the balcony, as the paparazzi apparently noticed.

"Yeah. *Safe* is the *last* word that comes to mind when I put 'Lightning Lex Lambert' and 'corporate sponsorships' in the same sentence," Jess elaborated. "I'm afraid your chances with Mr. Barker were tenuous before... but now they're shot to hell."

"Brett Barker can ride a knob straight to hell," I grumbled angrily, downing the rest of my ale.

"Yeah, well, he's your meal ticket," Jess shrugged. "You can't exactly antagonize the Head of Public Relations for the entire Patrovo Corporation and then expect to wind up his year's pick for the cereal boxes."

I gave a stiff nod to the bartender, who poured me another ale and rushed it to my side. "Cheers, mate," I offered him, and he stifled a small smile with utmost professionalism.

"You're my publicist, Jess," I told her after a quick, refreshing sip. "How do I get my big, grinning mug on a commercial?"

Jess sighed. "Do you want me to answer as your *friend,* or as your *publicist?*"

"Both, obviously."

"Well, as your *publicist,* you need to clean your fucking act up – and *fast.* No more of these stunts. The only reason you even have a ghost of a chance anymore is that the entire country bloody well loves you. You're a national icon, regardless of the pair of lips around your cock at any given moment. If you really want this sponsorship deal with the Patrovo Corporation… something's gotta give, and it's gotta give *now*."

I read her eyes thoughtfully, tempted to lash out about my various trophies, athletic stats, or how vital to pop culture I already was.

But I trusted Jess.

I *valued* her.

And as an old friend and a talented representative, I let her speak to me in ways that would earn scathing destruction under any other circumstances.

"So that's *Publicist Jess* speaking," I commented gruffly. "What about the other one?"

"As your *friend?*" Jess asked.

I nodded quietly.

Her eyes flashed wildly again, and that smirk slipped back across her lips. As I felt a heavy pit in my stomach, she leaned forward, whispering as if anyone could hear us in this private pub room.

"I think I have an idea…"

My skepticism somehow found a new height. "An idea, yeah?" I asked, crossing my arms. "Am I going to like this?"

"Well, that depends…" Jess mischievously remarked, taking another swig of her drink.

"How do a few weeks in America sound?"

"Why the bloody hell would I want to go to America?"

Jess slapped a hand down on the table. "Because in America, *nobody* knows your name."

Chapter 1

Riley

The canvas sang with streaks of color as I dashed my palette knife along the taut material. Beneath my deft strokes, a serene landscape was springing to life, filled with clouds, mountains, and trees… and for the foreground, a hilltop pasture.

This was what I lived for.

Painting came naturally to me. On my mother's side of things, a thick streak of artistic creativity ran in the family. My grandmother had been a skilled seamstress and designer. My mother had been particularly skilled in sculpting.

That left me: Riley Ricketts, the painter.

Happiness was an empty canvas and a broad spectrum of vibrant paints, all ready for the skillful dance of my wrist. I favored a water-based style, coating the blank vessel of my artwork with a thin layer of clear-coat before adding in the surreal colors with a palette knife, a half-inch brush, or the edge of whatever expendables I had nearby.

I'd painted with sponges, crushed chocolate wrappers, Lego bricks, even steel wool. A consummate improviser, I worked with whatever was accessible and necessary to achieve the effect.

Although the gift came almost as naturally to me as breathing, I'd found myself in a bit of a bind these last few months.

The magic had gone away.

Whatever invisible muse had been guiding my work, it had scampered off into the night. My art still came as easily as ever, but it felt uninspired. It never looked the way I wanted it to.

Despite the protests of my few close friends, I let each failed piece languish in the spare closet. They called it the *Closet of Doom.* It had become a graveyard of forgotten canvases... a tomb for failed passions.

I glanced down at the canvas before me now, seated comfortably on the easel. As I wiped clean the palette knife in my hand and lifted a blue-tipped brush, ready to enhance the clouds above, my hand hesitated waveringly.

No, I thought to myself.

This won't do.

As if I were a disappointed parent, I dipped the brush back into the cup of water and beat the Devil out of it against the metallic easel frame. Down went my pallet, set aside for later use, and the brush dropped into my easel-side container.

I stretched my limbs, intertwining my fingers outwardly above my head. The light was already turning, casting my small studio in the throes of twilight. Soon, Reiko would be here, ready to cast off another dismal day running her boss's sandwich shop. Maybe Connor would join us tonight, although I was growing less and less patient with his passive-aggressive advances.

It was obvious he wanted to date me, but I'd held the same sisterly affection for him that I had since junior high… for whatever reason, that apparently wasn't enough anymore.

Worries for another time, I decided, bending to the side to stretch my back.

I heard the door squeal open, and the slight clatter as it slid back into place.

"You in the studio?"

"Yeah. You can come in."

Reiko Sugiyama leaned against the doorway, already dressed in her street clothes. With a cute, round face and soft features, her casually fierce eyes reinforced everything that her sheer force of presence said: *Don't fuck with me.*

Despite her lithe form, Reiko's snarkiness and intimidation were the things of legend. I'd only ever witnessed it secondhand, but my *other* best friend since junior high was a sight to behold. There wasn't a single bone in her body that lacked confidence, and she walked with her head held high and a strut that showed the world who was really the boss.

It was a shame that she was so lazy.

With just a pinch more ambition, she would have already left her job: babysitting a bunch of teenagers barely able to string along a decent club sandwich.

"Whatcha got there?" Reiko asked, nodding in the direction of the canvas. "No, no, let me guess… another one of your recent failures, am I right?"

"Maybe," I answered apathetically.

"Yeah, I thought so," she sighed, pushing off from the doorway and sauntering over. Her black boots clanged against the hardwood floor as she bent over beside me and peered at the canvas. "You know, whatever it is that you *hate* about your art these days, I just don't see it. This looks just as fucking fantastic as your usual shit."

"*Shit* being the operative word," I replied, wandering towards the kitchen to give her privacy with the painting. After hours of being in the zone and away from my bodily needs, I was positively parched.

"You *know* what I mean!" She called out from the studio room. "I just don't get it. People would *kill* for talent like yours. Tell me, explain it to me... what makes this suck to you?"

Pouring myself a glass of water, I ripped the scrunchie from my hair. My mane fell over my shoulders, the unfurled locks eager for release.

"I don't expect you to get it," I answered truthfully. "There's something missing. A spark..." I walked back down the hall, settling against the doorway as she had before.

"Well, I'll trust your judgement," Reiko grinned over her shoulder, before her smile faded into concern. "But you've been on this warpath against your own work for, what, *months* now? I know you say you lost your spark or whatever, but maybe this stuff is better than you think?"

She turned back to the mostly finished landscape, clearly admiring my efforts. "I mean, this doesn't belong in your Closet of Doom. If that's what you're doing with it, let me put this up on my wall. I need art for my bare ass apartment anyway. Hell, I'll take half of that closet right now."

"You know I can't let you do that," I reminded her. "I can't let this out into the wild. It's fine here… where it's safe… at least, until I can figure out what's wrong with it, maybe clean it up."

"Yeah, yeah, I know…"

She looked a little glum, but I appreciated that Reiko understood my artistic selfishness. The idea of something inferior that I'd created with my own hand being *out there,* even on a close friend's wall… the idea bothered me.

Hell, Connor had tried to sneak off with one of my castaway closet paintings, and I'd furiously banned him from my apartment for two months. It had been a breach of my trust as a friend and an artist.

Reiko understood.

"Alright, well, I know there's no convincing you otherwise," she finally conceded, standing up straight. "Anyway, I like it. It's good."

"Yeah, yeah," I smiled.

"…Oh! I almost forgot the whole reason why I'm here!"

She grinned ear to ear, clasping her fingerless gloved hands together. "Get yourself cleaned up, woman. We're going to the French Quarter tonight."

"Oh yeah?" I tilted my head. "Why's that?"

"Because the guitarist in that band I like is a bartender down there, and he tells me that this rugged, British dude showed up a few days ago. He's been coming in every night since, mostly keeping to himself. I think you need a little something different, so you'd better get glammed up and get your flirt on."

Now *that* was intriguing.

"I don't know… Maybe I don't feel like going out tonight," I replied, trying to bury the little devil of excitement creeping up inside me.

"That's exactly why you need to get out. You've been holed up in this apartment trying to get your mojo back. Maybe you're looking for *spark* in all the wrong places," Reiko said, grinning mischeviously.

"And you think I'll find inspiration in some British guy's pants?"

"It worked the last time, didn't it?" Reiko laughed.

I wanted to protest, but she was right.

One of the more defining characteristics of myself, besides my penchant for painting, was that I was a total Anglophile. I religiously watched the *BBC America* channel, following such British staples as *Doctor Who* and *Sherlock*. I'd only been to England once on a summer's break, but it had confirmed my every suspicion:

I loved England.

I'd come back from that trip full of inspiration.

Everyone close to me knew that… and to hear that there was a British guy here in town who'd fallen into routine at a nearby bar… Maybe I was *due* a little fun…

Besides… This was our usual night to go barhopping. We'd skipped the last few when she'd been overwhelmed with work, and I hadn't really been myself lately. Knowing that the English card was on the table added a whole other layer of excitement.

"What makes you think that he's into someone like me?" I asked thoughtfully, casting her a look.

"Geoffrey tells me that this guy's been turning down the most sex-starved vapid chicks around," Reiko recalled. "Hell, he's wandered back out alone every damn night. Whether or not he scores later, there's no telling, but none of *them* are successful, award-winning artists… maybe he's into someone with a few brain cells?"

"What's he look like?"

"Why don't you just go find out for yourself?"

"Your guy must have told you *something,*" I insisted. "Dish out the details. Get me amped to get pretty and scope this guy out."

The door clattered open again, and I inwardly sighed. I knew exactly who it was, although Reiko didn't appear to hear the sound of encroaching footsteps.

"Fine, fine," Reiko conceded, thinking for a moment. "Usually comes in wearing a nice suit... sandy-brown hair, broad but streamlined build... handsome as fuck... that's all that the dude told me."

"Handsome as fuck? Did somebody call me?" Connor asked, poking his head through the door.

With his floppy hair and boyish good looks, enhanced by squared glasses, Connor completed our happy little triad. *If only he wasn't so obviously attracted to me,* I thought to myself as he flashed me a sly smile.

"Nah, wasn't describing you, bro," Reiko sneered playfully.

He shrugged off the retort. "Who else could it have possibly been?"

"Just this rugged, British dude down at the bar," she answered enthusiastically. "I'm trying to convince Riley that we need to go check this guy out, because seriously I think she might be able to score him."

I couldn't figure out if she was blissfully ignorant of his fixation on me, or if she was just effortlessly cruel, but Reiko offered this tidbit of information up with the giddiness of a schoolgirl.

"Oh, I see," Connor answered quietly, retreating into a stoic face. "Is he at our usual spot?"

"Sounds like it," I shrugged. "I figured it was worth a check. You up for tagging along?"

Connor looked crestfallen, but he bravely slapped on a smile. "Fuck yeah, I've been looking forward to this drink all goddamn day."

"Rough day at the record store?"

"Definitely. Ever since Bowie shuffled off the mortal coil, we've been sold flat out of his records. Meanwhile, we've been *swamped.*"

"Would have thought you'd like the business," I shrugged. "Aren't you having trouble making the lease some months?"

"Well, yeah," Connor grinned. "But it's just me and Tiana there during the day and, well, we're not staffed to deal with a glam rock god up and dying on us... if it's not people pissed that we've run out of his discography, it's people bugging us with a ton of questions about related artists..."

Overlooking the one-sided romantic fixation between us, I carried a lot of respect for Connor Carelli. While I was in some galleries and Reiko managed someone else's sandwich shop and followed around that band, Connor had chased his dream of owning a bonafide record store.

The location was shit, the parking was worse, and the place was held together with a barebones staff and a lot of improvised renovations... but Connor's little record shop was *his*. Not only that, but he'd developed a reputation for carrying a carefully curated selection of classic obscurities and important memorabilia.

"Just to let you know, the guy usually leaves around 9PM," Reiko cut in. "So, if we're going, we'd better get down there soon. Unless you think you can seduce him in half an hour, at any rate."

I glanced at the clock. Despite the fact that the sunlight outside was only just waning now, it was already 7:30 PM. "Fuck these summers and their long hours…" I muttered to myself. "You two make yourselves comfortable. I've gotta get changed."

"Don't forget, your head is a canvas!" Reiko reminded me. She was used to me completely forgetting to wipe the paint smears off and apply a little makeup. "Put that artistic touch to work and get your face on!"

"Yeah, yeah…" I smiled, pushing past them to dive around the corner and into my bedroom. I reached into wardrobe and snagged a couple of items – a nice dress, a decent belt, a few accessories...

As I whipped off my oversized tee and my pair of black leggings, I suited myself up for what could be an *interesting* night.

I scanned my face in the mirror, tugging over my makeup bag from the top drawer beneath my sink. A little foundation, some contouring, maybe just a little refined shape to my eyebrows… I had the time to put this together.

The sounds of some old sitcom played from the living room. Undoubtedly, Reiko and Connor had made themselves comfortable on my couch, chilling with the Netflix on my old Xbox. At least they were occupied.

"Alright, Riley," I whispered to myself as I lifted the first instrument of my quick, studious makeover. "He sounds like a catch, and he's looking for something…" I smiled confidently at myself in the mirror. "You are gertting your mojo back! You are getting *laid* tonight by a thick, British cock. Time to get on the war paint…"

Chapter 2
Lex

While I nursed a Newcastle, I quietly ignored the young piece of ass that was giggling loudly in my ear with her cute southern drawl.

Jess's idea had been great on paper.

In England, there's a fresh scandal waiting around every corner for you. Brett Barker wants someone wholesome, and spoiler alert, Lex: that just ain't you, you know?

You're not just a bad boy.

You're THE bad boy.

You've gotta chill the fuck out somewhere that nobody recognizes you. Lay low for a couple of weeks… maybe find yourself someone out of that damned life. Someone intelligent who can do more than just look good on your arm or your damn balcony.

You need to go to the one place where nobody knows your name… America.

It was true.

Nobody here had recognized me.

Nobody here knew my name.

I couldn't tell whether to be relieved or offended. Tellingly, I seemed to cycle between the two at any given moment.

Of course, people here were equally obsessed with football, but they were fixated *on the wrong one*. Over my drinks every night, I'd stared up at the screen as some talking heads loudly and bombastically speculated over sports footage on some asinine show called *SportsCenter*.

Needs a new name, I thought to myself. *I haven't once noticed them mention even a hint about the most beloved sport on the planet.*

So far, we'd been here a week.

It had been my idea to visit New Orleans. I figured, I could disappear for a little while, find one of those pretty Southern belles I'd heard so much about, and kick back and ride out the tabloid cycle.

No harm, no foul.

Jess had been less than enthusiastic about that prospect – she'd wanted to get me *away* from the party scene, not drop me smack dap into the party capital of the Western Hemisphere. But with a little convincing, she'd been onboard with it.

After all, she could drink her weight in wine, and New Orleans was a city rich with historical significance and culture. I wondered if there might really be some voodoo out in those swamps, and she was eager to at least check out the world-famous port city.

Now, I'd heard the stories of belligerent Americans and how raucous they could be, but I hadn't been prepared for the Deep South.It seemed that all there was to do down here was (a) drink, (b) drugs, (c) fuck, and (d) stare at the goddamn television.

And I had to stay away from almost all of those things on *this* little trip… Lay low, stay out of the news, and come back to the UK a kinder, gentler Lex… The kind of Lex who gets his face on a cereal box instead of a tabloid.

Not that it would surprise anyone if I cocked this up.

"So, are ya gonna buy me a drink, or what?" The blonde beside me drawled, snapping me away from my thoughts.

"Ah'll take a Bloody Mary, thank yew very much."

Maybe she'd be fun for the night, but getting caught with some slutty college student from the US would be a whole new scandal.

Jess would kill me.

"Yeah, piss off," I muttered absentmindedly, glancing lazily towards her.

She gasped indignantly, wheeling her hand back to slap me. I took the blow, my cheek wincing with pain. I growled menacingly under my breath as she took a step back.

"You're an asshole," She shouted.

"Don't hit me again," I retorted.

"Hey! What's going on here?" Some loudmouthed bucko stepped into view, his lustful eyes glued to this chick. "This guy givin' you a problem, darlin'?"

"Sure as shit is!" She looked proud of herself.

"Hey, you're that *foreigner,* ain't'cha?"

"Might be," I replied noncommittally.

"Hey! Fellers! It's a *Brit!*" He called out with that stupid fucking voice of his, as if I was some kind of novelty in this area.

Then again, this was New Orleans.

I probably *was* a novelty here.

I'm too conspicuous, I thought to myself. *I need to leave a smaller footprint, maybe stop going to the same bar every night... even if they do make the drinks the way I like 'em...*

There were some murmurings as another fuck got up. He was dressed in a plaid shirt, dusty jeans, and cowboy boots. A ten-gallon hat was perched above his face. As he waddled into view, I could see that over a quarter of the room was quietly watching us now.

Not really the kind of attention I wanted.

"I don't know how you treat the ladies in your part of the world, *pahd'ner*, but here in the U, S of A, we treat women with *respect*," he told me with some sort of misguided authority over me.

The guy looked to be in his upper forties, sniffling a bushy moustache as he carefully summed me up.

I almost laughed…

But I was supposed to be playing it quiet. Tearing up a bar in New Orleans wouldn't play well if I wanted that sponsorship back home.

"No offense meant, lady," I told her, turning to the bartender. "One Bloody Mary for the lady, and a round for the house."

I cast my eyes back on the girl. "I'm not buying you another drink, but I'm sure one of these *strapping* young lads would be happy to take my place."

The first guy looked thrilled at the prospect, and the scene quickly died down. Within moments, the two of them were seated at a spare pair of barstools down the counter, and the *pahd'ner* was ambling back with his drink at my expense, apparently satisfied.

There were still eyes on me, but I expected that now. I'd started to recognize some faces since frequenting this fine establishment, and no doubt I'd raised some eyebrows. Maybe they didn't know who I was, but they sure as hell knew I didn't belong.

"Thanks for not causing a scene," the bartender murmured quietly enough for only me to hear. "I know you're still getting acquainted with the local flavor, but Southerners are fiercely patriotic… one syllable off your tongue, and you stick out like a sore thumb here."

"Yeah, I've noticed," I nodded thoughtfully.

"Anyway, this one's on me," he grinned, popping the top and dropping a second Newcastle beside the first.

"Cheers, mate."

I noticed him glance over towards the door and grin knowingly. Since there was nothing better to look at in this place, I glanced over and spotted a trio that I didn't recognize.

The Japanese chick was returning his smile. She was clad in some hodgepodge blend of biker gear and punk rock attire. Her interesting fashion sense somehow came together cohesively, even if it was a tad much. *Who the fuck is she trying to impress?*

The scrawny chap with the shaggy curls and the glasses looked mildly uncomfortable. Dressed in a ragged jacket and torn jeans, he looked like a highly functioning vagabond of some sort. When he made eye contact with me he looked even *less* comfortable, which almost made me grin. Did I just catch a hint of recognition? Maybe I'd finally found the one soccer fan in the whole country. I was hoping I wouldn't bump into too many of those here…

My entire train of thought derailed as shaggy-head moved aside.

The bird between them stole the show.

I didn't really go for the brunettes, but there she was, standing tall and confident. Her black dress elegantly hung around her womanly hourglass shape. Those beautiful eyes caught my attention in a heartbeat. Her radiant face scanned the room for a moment, zeroing on me at the bar, and a small smile crossed her lips.

Well, what do we have here?

The Japanese one noticed me as well, and whispered something into her ear. Their mate looked none too pleased, and he placed a hand on her shoulder and started to say something.

Bad move, apparently.

She shrugged off his touch and turned, quietly ripped him a new one, and then broke away from the two of them.

By the time she slipped into the chair beside me, I was *thoroughly* intrigued. The other two found a small bar table in the corner, which gave them a great vantage point to watch whatever we were about to do.

"Say something," she told me.

"Excuse me?" I asked.

The mysterious young woman smiled. "That'll do. What is that, *Estuary?*"

I raised an eyebrow.

"You know your accents."

"Could say that."

Unlike the other locals, she seemed to have a more dignified tongue, even if her own accent faintly slipped through.

It was my turn to smile.

"Who the Devil are you?" I asked.

"My name's Riley," the woman answered, holding out a small hand. Without thinking, I took it into my own, feeling how soft and delicate it was within my much sturdier grasp.

"Charmed. Call me Lex."

"*Lex*," she repeated, trying out the syllable for herself against the backs of her teeth. "I like that. Short for "Alexander?""

"Naturally."

"Well, Alexander, just between you and me, would you like to know a secret?" She leaned in closer, watching my eyes. I couldn't help but play along with whatever this was.

"Go on, then."

Riley glanced around quickly, then whispered into my ear, as if she were telling me the most important secret in the entire world: "We're going to fuck tonight."

If there had been beer in my mouth, it would have sprayed across the counter. I took a quick, hard look at this woman who had sat down next to me, and I couldn't help but shake my head in surprise.

Or was it admiration?

"Awfully presumptuous, yeah? And what exactly makes you think that I'm taking you to bed?"

"I don't care what reason you pick," she shrugged nonchalantly, smiling as the bartender walked over. "I just know that it's going to happen." Her tone shifted. "Hi, could I have a glass of shiraz?"

"Certainly," the bartender nodded.

"Oh, and put it on his tab," she jabbed a thumb to me without turning her head. "If you'd be so kind, Geoff."

He glanced over for confirmation, and I was so impressed that I could only give a crisp nod.

The bartender poured a glass of wine for her, setting it down in front and giving a slight nod of acknowledgement. I returned the gesture and watched her take a quick sip.

"Delicious," she cooed.

Who the hell is *this woman?*

I was about to find out…

Chapter 3
Riley

Ok, maybe I'd been a little too forward, but this man was sex on wheels. His style, his eyes, his voice. I don't think I'd ever been more instantly turned on in my entire life. It wasn't longer than two hours of seductive, dominant coercion before my back hit the comforter of Lex's hotel bed, his strong kisses already littered across my throat and my lips.

The weight of his streamlined, hardened body slid down against mine. Effortlessly pinning me beneath himself, his lips found my neck, kissing hungrily into the soft flesh there.

I relented to the heat of his touch, allowing him to find purchase into my skin. His lips stained a trail of kisses along my collarbone, rising up the opposing side of my throat, and then there it was – his lips on mine.

My chest heaved beneath his might as I gave in, surrendering myself up for the taking.

The fine, strapping Englishman didn't ignore the impulse, sliding the straps of my dress over my shoulders, his rough hand clenching into my thigh as he kissed me deeply and passionately.

Even in that moment, I could feel something spark deep inside, but the very thought alarmed me. Instead, I pushed it aside, concentrating more on the matter at hand.

The matter, that was, of his cock.

I could already feel it yearning for me. The bulge trapped within the fabric of his trousers pressed outward for me, hungrily demanding satisfaction. As he shifted his weight above me, I could gather a more accurate sense of its size… it was an intimidating weapon, larger than any that I'd experienced before.

Oh, the heat that came off of it!

My fingers clasped for his belt beneath him, eager to rip that tool free from its fabric prison, but Lex grabbed my wrists and forced them back up.

Pinned on either side above me, he dove in for more, holding my captive form at the ready as his lips pressed into mine. His tongue slid across my own, inviting it to play.

And play it did.

He knew just how to kiss me properly, and I welcomed the wetness of his lustful tongue into my hungry mouth. The sheer *ferocity* of how he touched me took my developing lust and set it fully ablaze. Even now, he ignored the demands of my nimble fingers, restraining me instead of allowing them to coil around his throbbing cock.

"Just let me," I whispered between kisses.

His eyes flared open, filled with such a primal need that it almost terrified me. "No," he groaned, grinding himself between my legs to taunt me further.

"But I want to… I know you need it, too…"

A smirk flickered across his lips. "Not yet."

Oh good, I thought to myself. *This one's got a backbone. I can work with that.*

He released my wrists, but chose to slide down, whipping the dress up over my thighs. I sat up to help him as he whisked the garment clean from my body, leaving me in just my matched red bra and panties.

"You're gorgeous," Lex whispered, taking me in with hungry, borderline *ravenous* eyes.

"All just for you," I smiled naughtily.

With that provocation, he knelt on the bed between my legs, effortlessly casting the bra aside as his deft fingers unlocked the clasp. My ample bosom spilt forth, milky white breasts with perky little peaks. Already, my nipples stood at attention, swelling with anticipation for his touch... and in this regard, he certainly didn't disappoint.

As he pushed me back onto the bed, Lex descended down upon me. With a hand clasped around one breast, his tongue snapped around the erect nub. I moaned with content as he began lapping away hungrily at the darkened bump, his outstretched hand clasping around the other breast.

His tongue sent waves of shuddering pleasure down my skin, and my fingers naturally wove into his hair to keep him pressed tightly against me. Still disobeying, he took the opportunity to alternate positions, switching his sucking mouth to the other nipple. His fingers tightened around the freshly exposed nub, twisting and grazing it between the digits.

He knew just how to knead my bosom, too, squeezing hard, but not too hard; alternating pressure, approach, and any other conceivable factor.

My hands, discontent with holding his head, slipped down to wrap around the back of his neck. He murmured with satisfaction at this choice while continuing to please me.

Soon, he kissed a trail down my stomach to my thong, pressing his lips against the thin sheer of the fabric. The pressure hit just the right spot, as he had expected – my hands dug backwards into the comforter, and my back rose up from the bed.

"Ooohhh…" I murmured in delight, biting my bottom lip as he chuckled huskily, repeating the effort a second, then a third time…

And before I knew it, his thumbs had slid into the small lining, and he was whipping my thong clean off my thighs, around my ankles, and off to the floor with the dress.

"It's not fair, Lex," I whispered hungrily.

"What's that, love?"

"I'm completely naked for you, and you've still got everything on..." I grasped his tie, pulling his face down to mine. Our lips met, and I kissed him fervently, sliding my tongue along his own. "You'd better lose some of this..."

"Why don't you give me a hand, yeah?"

I sat up and knelt behind him as he sat on the nearby corner of the bed. My hands brushed along his blazer, sliding it off his shoulders and tossing it to the side. Reaching around his throat, I slowly, gradually undid his tie, sliding it up his dress shirt as I pulled it free.

Next, my hands wrapped around his arms, and I found and began unclasping his buttons. My lips dug into his neck, tasting of his throat as I slowly, gradually undressed this beautiful specimen of a man.

With the shirt free, that left only his slacks and socks. For a moment, I was distracted by the dark, intricate tattoos, hinting at something fierce beneath that skin...

Lex stood up in front of me, and I grew distracted. I began to unbuckle his belt, sensing the heated power of his tremendous cock. Just knowing how close it was drove me absolutely wild.

The mighty beast bulged against his boxer briefs as they came into sight. I was tempted to stop where I was, release the dragon, and try to get it into my mouth…

But Lex noticed this, and he urged me onwards. I continued pulling his slacks down until he stepped out of them, whipping off his socks, and standing confidently before me.

Lex was a sight to behold.

He stood just over six feet tall, with a broad, rugged and athletic build that was just stacked with sharp, incredible muscles. The rugged six-pack beneath his pectorals stretched down to the telltale "v", digging down to his cock…

A cock that was *huge*.

Who the hell was this guy? Everything about him screamed *confidence, experience, and eager to please*…

Besides the amazing body on this rugged foreigner, I was caught off-guard by the ink. Swirls of black tattoos stretched across his pecs and down his arms, stretching down towards his six-pack.

"Were those... *painful?*" I cautiously asked with abated breath, unable to rip my eyes from the fierce tattoos.

"Some," he chuckled, crossing his arms to show them off. "Obviously, the ones above my heart were the worst. The skin's rather tender there... do you like them?"

I had the worst case of cottonmouth I'd had in ages, and all I could do was nod curiously, my eyes still glued to their edges.

"Good..."

I realized too late that he was pushing me back in bed, coercing me backwards until I was comfortably lying in the pillows. His lips met my skin along my collarbone again, and he hungrily peppered a trail of kisses downwards, his fingernails digging into my skin and dragging down to clench above my thighs...

As he pressed into the creases of my hips, shouldering my thighs above his shoulders, his lips pressed into each thigh in succession. He stained them with kisses before pressing his face between my legs, his tongue immediately gracing my engorged clit and sending shivers down my spine.

"Oh, *Lex…*" I murmured with a moan.

He continued to pry the bead of my passion, his lips pressing against my wet sex. "You taste so good, love," he observed, his voice dripping with lust. "You're just what I wanted."

I nodded, lost in pleasure. He stroked my clit with his tongue once more, falling into a rhythm as he manipulated the tiny organ in ways no man had ever done to me before.

He knew when enough was enough, too, pulling back just as the button started to grow sensitive. His tongue stiffened as it pressed into my body, lapping away at my lower lips as he clenched his fingertips deeper into my thighs. In response, my legs tightened around his skull, and my back threw itself against the bed again.

"Oh god… Lex… *fuck…*"

My fingers threaded back into his hair as I rode his tongue, eager for release. His face kept pressing against the sensitive folds above my slickened opening, and it continuously pushed me to new heights.

He's just so fucking good at this, I thought to myself. *Holy shit, Riley, you finally found someone who knows how to get you off...*

True to form, it wasn't long before I could feel the distant rumblings of an impending orgasm. Whereas actually experiencing my own thrilling conclusion was a gamble every time, this man had brought my senses to a record-beating level, both in intensity and speed.

"Oh god... Lex... I'm gonna... don't stop, please don't stop... don't you *dare* fucking stop..."

My thighs tightened around his face as he amped up the rhythm, returning to suck my clit into my mouth.

I was putty in his hands then, and the shivers down my spine turned into pure, unadulterated nirvana. As pleasure whiplashed down my back, a jaw-dropping orgasm tore through me, tearing inhuman, animalistic groans from my lips.

"Fuck – Lex – I'm coming – just –
"

With staggered breaths, I moaned out a string of expletives, finally crumpling to a heap against the bed. He disentangled my legs from around his head, pulling himself up to plant a stained kiss against my lips.

My arms wrapped around him, pulling him deeper. I could taste the evidence of my own satisfaction on him, and our tongues danced together as I wiped it clean with my own.

"Who *are* you?" I found myself asking with a mixture of contentment and surprise at his skill. "I've never, *ever* been with someone this… talented…"

"Well, Lex Lambert isn't just *someone,* love," he chuckled knowingly. After a second, his face changed, and he realized he'd divulged his surname to me.

"…Forget I said that," he chuckled nervously.

"Why, is your name important?" I asked, glancing curiously at him. "Really though, now that you mention it… *who are you?*"

"Just someone passing through," he deflected casually, stroking his cock as he hovered above me. Supporting himself on one elbow, I could sense the power of his chiseled strength, and I knew that my window to press the matter was closing – and *fast*.

"Lex, you can tell me anything–"

The head of his cock pushed into me, parting the wet, yearning lips of my slick chasm around his generous girth.

"Wait – you're not wearing a condom –"

"Don't worry, love," he chuckled between groans. "I'm clean. I get checked every few weeks… and I had a vasectomy. If there's a kid happening, that kid's gonna be planned."

Every few weeks?

How much sex does this dude HAVE?

I felt his tremendous size pushing inwards, stretching my body and testing my limits.

All semblances of composure and concentration flew straight out the window. It was all I could do to keep my head as he thrust himself deeper inward.

"Oh *fuck me sideways*," I moaned. "There's *no way* this is gonna fit…"

"It's working out nicely so far," Lex chuckled, holding me down as he pushed another inch inside. "Go on, just relax… we're already halfway there, love…"

I adjusted my hips, spurred on his words.

"Come on, then," I murmured. "Let's do this."

With a cocky little grin, Lex pushed deeper. His rock-hard weapon pierced further into my trembling folds, pulling deep moans from my lips and forcing him to groan with intensity.

"*Fuck,* Riley, you're so goddamn *tight* around my cock…" He murmured with conviction. "I'm not even all the way in, yet. It's so hot inside…."

"You feel so good inside me," I cooed between moans, my fingers clenching into the bedding again. Truth be told, it felt like he was splitting me apart… but oddly, it was an intensely *satisfying* way to go. If he really did break me in two, it would be worth it. "Hold on a minute, please."

"Okay," he hurriedly responded, pausing in the onward march of his thick cock.

I gathered my breath and fought my body, forcing myself to relax a little more. Biting my bottom lip and closing my eyes, I thought of babbling brooks, rustling meadows in the wind, and the scent of the forests…

All imagery that helped me limber up and get into the zone of painting.

My eyes flew back open, and I nodded.

I was as relaxed as I was ever gonna be.

Lex slowly pushed further inside, tactfully retreating an inch whenever necessary, only to regain his ground and then some. Within a few more moments, I could feel him hilt himself against my hips, and I realized that I'd taken the entire cock into me.

"Oh *fuck,* Lex," I murmured with a gasp.

He pulled his hips back for a moment, and then pushed forward again, slowly easing me into a rocking motion. I gradually met and matched his rhythm, pushing myself to accept this tremendous rod of white-iron iron within my wet pussy, stretching my walls and pushing me to my very limits.

His hand clasped around my mouth, sealing my lips. In light protest, I tried to vocalize indignation, but he was already grasping my bare breast with the free hand, squeezing the supple flesh and teasing the erect nipple between his fingers.

The tactic worked, redirecting my attention as he lowered his lips to the other nipple. By deftly pleasing my exposed chest, he pushed a fresh flood of mounting sensations into my head – letting me ease into the rocking of our hips.

Thank god he was so tall.

My thighs spread a little further, and then I snapped my ankles together, clasped around his hips. My heel nestled into the small of his back as I kept him close, tightly controlled against my body.

Meanwhile, his lips found mine, crushing against me as he steadied himself with his forearms locked down on either side of my shoulders. I coerced him to move them closer, and he constrained me between them, binding both of us together for this carnal throe of pleasure.

His hips began to pick up the tempo, and I grew accustomed to his speed. I was just relaxed enough to enjoy the sensations, and my legs wrapped around him kept Lex from jackhammering into my sopping wet pussy with that unfathomable tool of his.

He really will *tear me apart if he does that,* I thought to myself briefly…

But it was hard to cling to any reasonably sentient thoughts as I became overwhelmed by his power. Lex held me down beneath him, carefully but powerfully thrusting into my body, again and again…

Moans escaped my lips, and my strength began to sap from my limbs. I realized that my fingernails had been digging into his shoulders tightly.

I released my grip, letting my whitened knuckles return to their natural, pinkish color. Meanwhile, my ankles slipped apart, and I steadied myself beneath him as he fucked me.

But Lex grew tired of this position, and soon I was forced onto all fours in front of him. His fingers pressed against my folds, one slipping in to test my chasm.

"You're still so wet for me, Riley," my partner groaned with gratification. "I love how much you want this."

"That's right," I cooed, wiggling my hips just a little. My eyes widened as he began to stroke that huge cock, and I hastily added: "Just be gentle, okay?"

"You don't want gentle," he answered, his smirk telling me everything about his levels of confidence… or was it *arrogance* at this point?

"I do at first," I insisted. "If you tear me in half, you realize that you won't be able to fuck me again, right?"

"A valid point," he added quickly, pressing the crown of his head into my folds. I turned back around, steadying my hands. One pressed out flat against the headboard, while the other squeezed the top.

Thinking quick, I moved it out before my fingers were crushed, flattening my palm across the top and the wall.

It was a good thing that I did.

I felt his cock surge halfway into my yearning pussy, and I screamed out the only syllable that I could grasp: "*FUCK!*"

"We have not yet even *begun* to fuck, Riley," Lex whispered in my ear as he bent over my ass. With a slight nip, he tugged the lobe between the teeth, then nestled his lips into my ear:

"But after this… you'll never be able to call another piss-poor shag a proper *fuck* ever again…"

Chapter 4

Lex

When my eyes flickered open the following morning, something felt different.

An arm… over my chest…

The events of the night flooded back into my memory banks, and I remembered the boastful upstart that had wandered into the pub and taken over my entire evening.

Here she was – *Riley*, I recalled quickly – fast asleep and curled up beside me.

As I let myself play back through the roulette of positions we'd experienced, long into the night, I drew a quick and effective conclusion…

It had been a rather satisfying evening.

I allowed myself to stare at the ceiling for a few minutes as I felt her chest rise and fall with her deep, slumbering breaths.

This was the first time that I'd been self-conscious of this small, rather quaint hotel room. Against Jess's desires,

I'd insisted on renting something small and unassuming… after all, I didn't want to call any attention to myself while I was here. She could have picked another hotel a few streets over, but as my publicist, she'd insisted on rooming nearby.

She settled for a floor down.

Jess was used to living to a certain standard of living. It came with the territory when you represented some hefty clients, including one of the biggest sports stars in the entire world. Luckily for her, the others were rather low-key, never causing a whole lot of trouble for her representation.

I was handful enough to make up for that.

But now, I somewhat regretted this decision. It was my nature to want my sexual conquests to wake up and see the extravagance in which I lived. Of course, I was going to just kick them straight out, but I liked to leave an impression.

I could feel Riley murmur against me now. She deserved some rest after the night that we'd had together. After all, once she'd grown a little more accustomed to my size, she had become surprisingly voracious.

It was difficult for her to keep up with me, but damn, did she try. All that pent-up energy from being away from my training had reflected itself into our time between the sheets.

For the first time in ages, I actually felt like getting back to work... After that marathon of sex last night, I could stand to do some sprints, knock out some *leg day*, or even just swim some laps and streamline my athletic build a little more.

A bothersome thought occurred to me.

It dawned on me that I hadn't heard from Jess since the late afternoon. However, my phone had buzzed a several times during my wild coupling with my new friend here, Riley.

I reached for my phone, unlocking it with a few button taps, and then...

The knocking at the door drew my attention. *Didn't I put a "Do Not Disturb" on the door? Is this the kind of service to expect at a* layman's *hotel?*

The knocking resumed, harder now.

"Lex? Lex, I know you're in there!"

Riley shifted around in her sleep slightly, and then her eyes darted open. "Who is that?" She sleepily asked, and I groaned my response.

"That would be Jess."

She looked at me inquisitively, but I didn't think anything of it at the time. Instead, I ascended from the bed, tossing on a pair of boxers and my pajama bottoms.

With Riley's eyes on me as she drew the bedding up to her neck, I lazily sauntered over towards the door and unlocked it.

"Lex, you idiot! Why haven't you been answering my—"

I slid into position to block Riley from sight, but Jess had already seen her. Glancing over my shoulder, she looked at me with a mixture of surprise and disappointment.

"Lex, what the fuck?"

"I met her yesterday," I responded sleepily. "She spent the night."

"Yeah, I can obviously see that... hell of a night for you to pick, though," Jess crossed her arms, a telling smirk plastered across her face. "I've been trying to catch you for hours…"

"Why, what is it?" I asked curiously.

Jess was always bad at hiding her emotions. Disappointment, maybe even fear, clouded her expression almost immediately. She took a deep sigh, and I knew the following news couldn't be good…

I heard rustling from the bed behind me. I'd almost forgotten about last night's lay, and for a little privacy, I held the door ajar and stepped partially out.

"Out with it!" I hissed the demand.

Jess's expression hardened – and then I *knew* the news was going to slay me. "A friend of mine in the agency says that Brett Barker is already considering… *alternate* possibilities for the latest contract."

My blood ran cold.

"Who?"

"My source itself is reliable, but the information… we're not exactly–"

"Not *another* word that doesn't answer the fucking question," I told her in no uncertain terms. "We both knew this could be a possibility. So tell me… *who is it?*"

Jess took a deep breath.

"Alistair Pritch."

My heart plummeted into my stomach. Pritch was a defender on our team, and a fiercely competitive one at that. His role was to protect the goalie and ensure that the football didn't *dare* progress into the goalkeeper's box… and he was very, *very* good at it.

He was also my singular proper rival in the sport – the one person who kept me on top of my game by sheer necessity.

"Pritch…" I responded blankly.

"That's right," Jess bit her bottom lip. "Alistair Pritch is in the running. My source tells me that he's the favourite contender for the contract."

It wasn't just a simple rivalry between players. The National Team drew in the best football players from the entire country, from various leagues and teams. It just so happened that his and my teams were, for most of our careers, bitter rivals through and through.

The goal for the National Team, as with *any* represented country, was to blur oppositions and contests to string together the best of the best.

Of which I was the king.

But Alistair... Alistair Pritch was the wicked chancellor to my reign. A viper in the grass, he followed orders and obeyed my directions... so long as there wasn't any foolhardy alternative that would propel himself into the spotlight.

The crowd loved him, too. I might be *Lightning Lex Lambert,* but the world knew Alistair Pritch as *The Renegade.* Pritch was clever; his disobedience was a wildcard for my game plans, but he made decisions that I had to begrudgingly call sound. He'd never make it look like he was actively rebelling against me – it was always a spur of the moment, completely reflexive maneuver.

And it had helped win more games than I was willing to admit. Pritch was always keeping me on my toes, and always forcing me to stay sharp.

Our rivalry was legendary.

And now he was trying to rip my contract out from under me before I could even sign a page.

"I'm going," Riley muttered as she pushed past me into the hallway, fully dressed. I could only give a distracted, dumbfounded nod as she disappeared around the corner and stormed off.

What the fuck is her *problem?* I thought to myself absentmindedly. *I just got the worst fucking news of my week...*

"So, who the hell was *that?*" Jess asked curiously, glancing down the direction my partner for the evening had disappeared.

"That was... Riley," I commented.

"Oh yeah? Why the sudden change? Thought you were going to lay low and, you know, *avoid* causing any sort of scandal while you were here..." She side-eyed me with a grin as I led her back into the hotel room. "Just couldn't keep it in your pants, yeah?"

"It was a little different from that," I recalled apathetically, still sucker-punched by this new tidbit of information.

Alistair Pritch, of all fucking people? Although, it made *sense*, in a way that made my blood boil...

"Oh yeah? Different *how?*"

I didn't give any thought to the answer, which is probably why it was a particularly honest, straightforward one.

"Riley impressed me."

"She... *impressed* you?" Jess seemed shocked. "This is new. Impressed you *how*, exactly?"

"The girl had no idea who I was, and she took charge," I thought aloud. "Such unwavering confidence. The girl knew how to stir me up, and she kept me on my toes."

"And you just let her scamper off like that?" Jess asked, cocking her head to the side.

"What are you getting at?"

My best friend shrugged. "I don't know. For a minute there, it *almost* sounded like you *respect* her."

"Maybe I do," I answered noncommittally.

"Doesn't sound like any *Lightning Lex Lambert* that I know," Jess chuckled, pulling out a chair from under the obligatory writing desk and seating herself.

"Yeah, well. Maybe I'm trying on something new," I answered, stepping into the bathroom to wash my hands in the sink. I raising my voice over the hot, running water. "You know. Seeing how I like it."

"Well, pissing off your *something new* isn't such a good idea!" She called out loudly from the other room.

"What do you mean, *pissing her off?*" I asked, wiping my hands clean with a stiff, rough hand towel as I strolled back into the main room.

"What, you didn't see that look on her face?" Jess sharply took in a breath for emphasis. "She was *livid.* Doesn't surprise me, though…"

"You're speaking cryptically," I simmered. "You know that I don't like *cryptic*. Get on with it."

"How does it look to you?" She asked. "She's half-asleep, all cuddled up to you or whatever, and then some strange woman answers the door. You get up, you get into some hushed, heated conversation, all mysterious and shit, and then when she tries to make a show of storming off, you just let her? You realize that she was mad, and you didn't even *bother* trying to stop her."

I didn't like the sound of that.

"That's not what it was at all."

"*Context,* Lex," Jess shook her head. "She doesn't know who you are… unless you told her."

"Didn't tell her a thing,"

"Right. So, she doesn't know who *you* are… she doesn't know who *I* am… and she's totally in the dark as to the secrecy. Hell, it probably looked like I'm some jilted ex-wife or some shit, coming to bother you."

I hadn't considered that.

"Fuck me," I grumbled.

I glanced down at my pajama pants.

"I'm… not exactly equipped for this right now," I muttered. "You're my publicist. Go catch her."

"I barely saw the chick," Jess shrugged. "Besides, I wouldn't know where to start. I'm not exactly private eye material, you know."

Grumbling, I pulled upon my wardrobe and whipped out a few choice garments. "Fine. I'll handle it. If I'm lucky, she might come to me."

"You think so?" She asked, that mischievous smirk on her face again. "I dunno…"

"If not… there was a Japanese girl who wandered in with her last night. I've seen the bartender speaking with her from time to time – I think they're friends. I can probably follow up on that lead and track her down, but only if I have to. I don't want to force it, after all."

Dwelling on these thoughts, I buttoned up my long-sleeved top, swapped the pajamas for slacks, and whipped a blazer over my shoulders. My publicist made and poured herself a cup of coffee, and then spat it out in my bathroom sink.

"Ugh! This is *fookin'* disgusting!"

"There's that *chav* coming out," I teased.

"Don't you start with me," Jess squinted an eye and gave me a defiant glare. "You *know* I'm not a damned, dirty *chav*."

"Could've fooled me."

She looked like she was going to burst a blood vessel, but relaxed. I recognized that look – she was deep in thought, considering something that we'd both overlooked.

"What is it?" I asked, stepping back into view. I was suited up and ready to tackle the day, even if that involved tracking down a wayward lay to straighten out some things.

After all, the sex had been pretty good...

And Jess was right.

It really had been a long time since someone had impressed me.

"This overnight woman of yours, this... damn the gods, what was her name again?"

"Riley."

"Right," Jess continued. "Thanks. This *Riley*. You said you found her challenging. Would you say you stand by that assessment?"

I straightened my tie in the mirror.

"I think so."

"She could be the answer you need."

I paused. "...Go on."

"What does Alistair Pritch have that you don't, Lex? Really think about that for a moment. What makes him *way* more attractive than you for a corporate, multi-million sponsorship?"

"Choose your words carefully," I growled.

"I'm not trying to stir you up," she smiled. "Apply those critical thinking skills of yours. *What does he have that you don't?*"

I begrudgingly considered her question.

"His record is weaker... but he's a maverick on the field... he's a defiant upstart, a wildcard, but a highly-calculating–"

"You're looking at the wrong details," she coerced me. "Think about his *stability.*"

"What are you getting at?" I demanded, whirling around to stare at her. "Do you have a plan, or not?"

Jess smiled at me softly, the way one would at an adorable pet. I didn't like it. "Pritch has a wife," she responded. "A wife and a kid. He's got a solid family, and that carries through to his reputation off the field. None of these playboy scandals of yours... he's clean. Squeaky clean."

"What's that got to do with anything?"

"Everyone knows you're the better player Lex, but he's a *safe* bet," Jess commented.

"And that's what Brett Barker wants," I growled, driving a fist into the wall. I could feel it slightly give way beneath my pressure. "He wants a safe bet. No scandals, no fuck-ups."

"That's right. He's going to choose Pritch over you because you're the loose cannon football star." Jess threw her hands up as she spoke. "Sure, you have the prestigious record, the respect, and the wins under your belt... even if the National Team hasn't won the World Cup beneath your leadership."

"The National Team hasn't won a World Cup since 1966," I clarified.

"Oh, I'm not saying you aren't a capable leader, by any means," she backtracked. "But you haven't given him that hole-in-one. You've been National for, what, three years now? If you'd led the team to international domination, that'd be one thing..."

"Not everyone on the team is as good as me."

Jess caught the primal, irritated tone beneath my voice. "Be that as it may... we'd be having a *very* different conversation right now if they were. Instead, the Head of Public Relations needs to make the wiser choice for corporate sponsorship.

"Sounds like both of his highly-qualified options are: the popular, arrogant playboy, practically a force of destruction both on the field and off... and the defiant but grounded, beloved subordinate, who is *still* a pop culture icon and a member of the National Team.

"Who's he logically going to pick?"

I grit my teeth.

"*Unless* you show him something else."

"Something like Riley."

"That's right," Jess schemed. "No more of these ridiculous one-night stands, public intoxication feats, and making my job a living *nightmare*," she told me. "You've got to settle down. Find yourself a nice girl. An *American* could work... it's an interesting but believable choice for you. Someone who challenges you… someone who can keep you in line."

"And I have to marry her?"

"Of course not!" Jess laughed. "But getting a girlfriend out of her is a step in the right direction, wouldn't you think?"

I dwelled on this a little longer.

"You think it's her?"

"From the way you went all googly eyes when we were talking about her?" Jess asked, standing up from the chair and straightening out her outfit. "She's a girl you sound like you actually *respect*. I think she's a probably a good start."

Chapter 5
Riley

Unsurprisingly, the English guy had turned out to be an arrogant prick.

And the sex had been phenomenal…

Isn't that how it always worked?

It wasn't all bad… It's just a shame that I didn't have a chance to cut my proverbial tether and bolt before the woman showed up.

I wasn't sure who she was.

A wife?

A girlfriend?

It didn't really matter. I'd gathered up my things and just pushed my way out the door and the asshole didn't even try to stop me.

It wasn't hard to navigate down to the ground floor and out the door. He was staying at one of the halfway-decent hotels in the area, and within a couple of minutes I was already on my way back home to my apartment.

Oh well, I thought to myself. *At least I got myself a great fuck in there before the sky came crashing down.*

The further away from the hotel I walked, the more that I considered the night. It had been more than just sex. Lex had pushed me to my very limits. The Englishman knew just how to excite me in the best ways, ramping up my passion before letting me dangle precariously at that precipice... letting me drift back... and then pushing me again and again, teasing me, until I finally begged for release.

When the release came, it crushed me.

I didn't reveal the fact, but I experienced my first multiple orgasm that night. Most guys hadn't really been particularly useful in the orgasm department, either finishing too quickly or not at all... but it was rare that I got to ride the climax myself.

With Lex, I'd lost count of the amount of times he'd thrown me over the cliff.

He was so brutishly rugged, and then there was that English charm of his. Every breath of his accent excited me, forcing me to hang upon his every last syllable. When he asked me to come for him, I couldn't help but oblige... and my fingernails had dug into his skin, riding out the intense heat between us.

And then he came inside me. It was the most incredible feeling in the world…

"Oh fuck," I thought aloud.

I came to an actual stop on the sidewalk and considered the implications. *What if he had been lying?* I thought to myself. *He told me that he was clean, and that he'd had a vasectomy… I had completely believed him without question.*

What the fuck, Riley?

So maybe I wasn't the first girl who made a mistake like that… I was better than this! I'd just cross my fingers and get myself tested. How did I let this happen?

I continued strolling back towards my apartment. After twenty more minutes of walking, I was ascending the stairs up to my humble abode and clicking the key through the keyhole.

It was time to see if my little taste of England had worked for my creative side… For the rest of the day, I decided to try painting. I needed something special if I wanted any chance of earning the attention from the one woman in the world who's opinion really mattered…

Gloria Van Lark.

Van Lark was a legend in the museum world. As the head curator for the *Spinnoc* museum in San Diego, she was known for her tall, hawkish appearance and her fiercely volatile temper.

This was a woman who was not to be trifled with, and who took her time very seriously. Just obtaining enough of her attention for an audience got you accepted into a number of distinguished museums around the country.

Then, there was the significant hurdle of *actually impressing her.*

Gloria Van Lark didn't care for resumes and histories. The fact that I had been gifted with an artistic scholarship to Finland, allowing me to take a full year to pursue an isolated artist's retreat, would mean precisely *nothing* to her.

Neither would the gamut of smaller museums that *already* carried some of my work, or the fact that I'd been fully supporting myself through my painting since I was a young teenager.

All that Van Lark cared about was the final product. After all, that was all that her clients and customers would see. It was probable that none of them would know these pieces of trivia about me, not unless I wound up with an exhibit, somehow…

But *that* was wishful thinking too high for even *my* lofty dreams. Exhibits were mostly reserved for dead artists… And I was still very much alive.

I found it hard to concentrate on the painting with my thoughts wrapped up in my irritation with Lex, and my fears that Gloria would never consider my work…

After blowing the entire day trying to focus on three different paintings — a beach at sunset, a forested mountain at night, and a small child crying – I eventually gave up on the prospect. Instead, I tossed my pallet down in frustration, washed my brushes, and kicked it back onto the couch.

It was starting to get late in the day. I realized that I hadn't eaten anything, and I thought about seeing if Reiko or Will wanted to grab a bite to eat.

I vetoed Connor immediately, on account of how standoffish and jealous he'd been about the Englishman at the bar. It had been clear from the start that he was passive-aggressively furious about the perceived competition.

I really didn't like that.

As for Reiko... I remembered that she was closing the sandwich shop tonight and working late on some payroll issues. She'd had to fire her assistant manager for trying to steal money, and that meant going through the finances and double-checking *everything*, just to be sure.

Oh yeah... she'd be doing *that* all night.

I made myself a quick sandwich to tie myself over, flicked on the Netflix, and then watched a few episodes of one of the millions of shows I was way behind on. By the time I was about done with that, it was getting pretty late, and I needed to decide whether to cook, order delivery, or venture out and grab a bite.

I decided on the latter.

Halfway towards the local Lebanese place, I felt drawn back towards the bar. I tried to ignore the sensation, knowing what was probably waiting for me there, but as I sat down and unwrapped my chicken shawarma dinner, the compulsion stood its ground.

That's why, after I finished my dinner, I decided to say *fuck it* to myself and mosey over a few blocks. With a little bit of luck, I'd just pop in and out, and then immediately move on with the rest of my life.

I wasn't that lucky.

As I'd expected, Lex was sitting at the bar in his usual spot. Some woman in a fancy dress was sitting next to him, laughing away and putting her hand on his shoulder.

I almost turned and walked out…

But he shrugged his shoulder free, glancing away. I could tell that he wasn't particularly enjoying her company, but she wasn't taking the hint. It was only when he leaned in with a cruel smile on his face and muttered something that she understood, pulling away indignantly.

She slapped him across the cheek, rising up from her chair and storming off.

Well… now or never, I guess.

Before someone else could try their luck, I sat down next to him. He looked honestly surprised, doing a brief double take before finally settling back into facing forward, both hands around his tumbler of liquor.

"What will you have?" He asked.

"Bloody Mary."

He gave a crisp nod to the bartender, who wandered over our way. A few minutes later, he was dropping off a glass at my fingertips, filled with a delicious concoction of vegetable juices and liquor.

"Thanks," I nodded towards the bartender in appreciation. He offered a quick smile before stepping away to take another order.

"I'm glad you came," Lex told me, still facing forward. I could see his fingertips slide further around the glass, constraining it within his grasp.

"Who was that woman from earlier today? The other one of you with the English accent?" I asked suddenly.

"That was Jess."

"Jess…" I traced the syllable with my lips. "Is she your wife?"

He actually laughed, breaking his composure to cover his eyes with his hand. "Never in a million years," Lex smiled softly.

"Girlfriend, then?"

"Jess enjoys a good power complex. She only dates the younger folk… expendable idiots who can keep her attention for a brief while, before she inevitably expels them," he chuckled. "Jess is the best damn friend I'll ever have, but that's all that we will ever be."

"Oh," I murmured.

It hadn't occurred to me that she might be anything less than his lover, and I suddenly felt rather silly in the head. It wasn't a sensation that I enjoyed, although I knew that I deserved it this time.

"So, what is she, then? *Old friends?* What's that supposed to mean?"

"She's *sort of* my agent."

"Your agent? What are you, a movie star?"

"I'm not a movie star," he replied, sipping from his drink. "I play football."

"Football? In England?"

"It's not *your* football," he mentioned offhandedly. "You'd call it *soccer*. But to the rest of the world, what I play is called *football*."

"I see," I replied.

"You sound disappointed," Lex observed.

"You're one of those meathead sports players," I told him. "I could never stand athletes. They're always just so full of themselves. Always thinking they need to dominate everything around themselves."

Lex thought on that for a moment, but he didn't respond, which I found rather telling.

"So, what are you doing in America, then?" I asked, surprised that I even really cared. "You're a long way from England."

"Just passing through."

"I think you mentioned that before," I recalled. "And you brought your agent? On a quick jaunt through New Orleans?"

"She can never turn down a good trip. Always loves to get out of England as often as she can. She has to stay close to me, especially when I'm playing internationally."

He suddenly looked disappointed with himself, as if he'd fumbled and revealed some major detail to me.

"You play other countries?"

"Sometimes," he responded coolly.

"Well, you must be a big deal, then."

Lex smiled wistfully. "Nah… just a guy."

We sat in silence for a moment, sipping from our drinks while we thought on things.

"I heard something about a contract this morning. What kind of contract?"

"Just some promotional thing," Lex replied absentmindedly. "Jess swung by to tell me that there's another player that's in the running for it, so I might miss out on it."

"Is it important?" I asked.

He chose his words carefully.

"It's very important to me."

I didn't particularly understand, but I nodded anyway. It seemed like the appropriate thing to do, given the circumstances.

"So, what do *you* do?" He asked.

"I paint," I answered noncommittally.

"You paint? Any good?"

"A little," I told him modestly.

He nodded, and the silence resumed between the two of us. I was starting to regret coming back here and seeing him again...

"I was given an academic scholarship for painting when I was younger," I eventually added. "Had the opportunity to go on an artist's retreat... holed myself away in a cottage in Finland for a year to study myself and my craft."

"That's interesting," he replied, turning his gaze to face me. "You must be plenty good to score something like that."

"Maybe I am," I confidently told him. "I've been selling my own paintings since I was fourteen. A couple of years later, I was supporting myself entirely through my artwork."

"Have anything up in the galleries?" he asked.

"Lots of my older stuff. My work is hanging in a dozen galleries here in town, including some of the more respected museums. I'm a little harder to find outside of Louisiana, but some places carry my work. Some state museums in New England, a few places out west… last count? Upwards of a hundred galleries carry at least *something* of mine."

Lex considered this. "That's impressive, Riley. Now that you mention it, I can see you sitting in front of an easel… You're good with your hands…"

"Thanks," I answered noncommittally, giving him a sideways glance and a bit of a smirk.

"So, what do your parents think of that?" He asked, casting me a studying glance as he sipped his glass of beer.

"My parents… aren't exactly part of the equation," I shrugged, holding back the emotions.

"Oh," he commented. "I'm sorry to hear it. I don't want to drudge up any painful memories…"

"My mother left when I was very young," I told him, surprising myself. "As for my father, he died in a motorcycle accident a couple of years later.

"I can't possibly imagine," he sympathized.

I continued on. "I passed through foster care for a while until a family took me in. They supported my art, and were proud of me... but they were Ivy League material, and I wasn't. When I decided to not follow in their footsteps, things got a bit... messy. So, when I came back from Finland, I was able to scrounge myself up a decent place to live, worked on my art, and here I am."

He nodded, reflecting on these words. "You're not in contact with them?"

"I have a phone number for my mother that may or may not work," I offered. "My biological mother, I mean. The last time we chatted, it turned into a massive argument. I haven't bothered with her in years.

"As for my foster parents, no. I burned the bridge. I'm on my own... just how I like it. Not having to rely on anybody but myself."

"You enjoy your solitude."

"I enjoy being in control of my life," I clarified. "It's a rewarding feeling to not need to depend on the kindness of others. I get what I need from people, offering them a little of myself in return, and then that's that. Besides my couple of friends, of course."

"The two from the other night. The Japanese girl and the thin, skittish guy."

"Yeah, Reiko and Will. I've known them since we were kids… since before I began supporting myself. The two of them have been there from the beginning."

"They sound like strong friends."

"The only people I can rely on."

I ordered another drink on his tab, and we drank together in silence for a few minutes.

"What about *your* parents?" I asked him.

Lex stiffened in his barstool. "House fire. Took 'em both when I was fifteen. I wound up on the streets, just a year shy of being a legal adult in England. I learned some street smarts, how to fight, things like that. Learned how to survive. If I hadn't been mindlessly dedicating myself to football, I'd probably still be there…"

"You were homeless?"

"For a while, yeah. Streets of London are a cold place…"

I thought on this carefully. "I couldn't possibly imagine what that's like, either."

"It's *bloody* tough, is what it is," Lex grumbled. "But I made it out, and with an appreciation for earning things. I've *earned* where I am in the world now. You might think that I'm just off globe trotting, but I'm here for a particular reason… and just enjoying my time while I can."

"And what reason would that be?" I asked.

Lex's lips curled into a mischievous grin. "Keeping myself out of trouble, little lady."

I couldn't ignore the fact that he was intriguing… or that the sex had been amazing. What I was doing here, I wasn't exactly sure… but I felt drawn to him.

Lex had a special kind of magnetism to him, and whatever it was, it cast a spell on me, tugging me closer and closer… *Is this a mistake? Should I just get the fuck out of here right now?*

I felt as if the decision was a conscious one, a fork in the road laid out ahead of me. I couldn't seen what lay down either direction, but something kept pulling my attention down one in particular…

Lex seemed to sense this.

"Listen," he murmured, turning to face me quietly. "Last night was a lot of fun, and I'm glad to see you back again. I want you to come home with me again."

"That's rather forward," I observed over the lip of my drink, taking a small swig.

"I thought you preferred to cut to the chase after last night," he reminded me. It was true, and I couldn't help but recognize how he was taking charge, sensing my apprehension.

"I can't offer you stability right now. I don't represent consistency or firm, solid ground. But what I *can* offer you is this: if you accompany me back tonight… if you choose to spend more time with me… you'll never have a dull moment. Whatever boredom is in your life, I can make that all disappear."

I eyed him silently.

His lip curled up into a smile again. "Well?"

I downed the rest of my drink and sat it down in front of myself, sliding my thumb and index fingertip along the glass, rotating it lightly beneath my touch.

"…Alright. Let's get out of here."

His smile turned practically devilish, and he clicked his fingers for the bartender. A few minutes later, and we were wandering down the streets of the French Quarter again, sauntering arm in arm towards his hotel room.

Until…

"*Bloody hell*," Lex muttered to himself, patting his pockets. "Dammit. I think I left my card in the bar…" He glanced over at me sheepishly. "Would you mind coming back with me for a moment?"

"I can wait here," I answered.

He sized up the surroundings for a moment. "Are you certain? This doesn't seem a fantastic part of town…"

I threw him a sideways glance.

"Okay, okay then," Lex grinned, his palms held up. "You live here, you can take care of yourself. I get it. Just wait here… I'll be right back."

The English gentleman grinned, shaking his head lightly before wandering back towards the pub.

I leaned against the wall of a nearby stoop, crossing my arms and tapping my foot. My mind wandered, wondering how I might paint my surroundings.

Effortlessly, I took in the details of the French Quarter. Not a whole lot of people were out; the few stragglers along the pavement were isolated into pairs or small groups from one another, with the odd speck of a person wandering around between them. None of them had any major defining features, which pleased me.

That would make for broad strokes, I considered to myself. *Put the emphasis on the buildings, and paint some ghosts to meander alongside them…*

The overall lighting was dim but poetic, casting bright bursts of light in front of bar fronts and under the occasional streetlight. I enjoyed the darkness that stretched between these parts, hoping to encroach across the area… but it was never enough to blacken the French Quarter.

There was such history here, and so many drunken escapades that no book could ever hope to properly catalogue them. New Orleans was such a wistful place, so full of life and light, even in the dark…

Lex still wasn't back. I was starting to grow somewhat impatient. *He said that he'd only be gone a couple of minutes… what's* taking *him?*

That's when I felt the firm hand, clasping over my mouth. Before I could even scream, I was being dragged backwards into an alley, away from the light, and a cocked gun pressed into my temple.

"Scream, and you die," a gruff voice told me. "Do you understand? Not even a fucking peep."

I nodded, and the hand slipped off of my lips… only for someone else to shove a gag into my mouth, tying it around my head.

Purely out of fear, I started trying to smack or punch whoever my aggressors were. I saw a quick glance – there were two of them, both dressed like thugs. My hands were restrained, and a blindfold was tied around my eyes.

"Mmmf!" I exclaimed, but it was useless.

I was being dragged backwards through the alley, stumbling blindly along with them. They were leading me away from the street, forcing me to follow them into the dark…

Oh god, no, not like this, I sobbed in my head.

Suddenly, my palms were slapped against the brick wall, and my legs spread. A pair of vicious, hungry hands tugged at the bottom of my dress, whipping it up over my hips…

"Mmm, such an uptight little bitch," one of the thugs chuckled. "Wonder if that pussy is this tight, too…"

"One way to find out," the other commented directly into my ear. He was the one assaulting my dress, and I just waited for the sound of ripping fabric as I struggled to fight my way out of this.

This can't be happening, I pleaded into my head. *I should have just fucking gone back with him to the bar. Oh god, they dragged me back here, he won't find me…*

"Oh shit, this bitch is wearing a thong!" The aggressor holding me pinned chortled quietly. "Well, *luck be a lady tonight…*"

I felt my thong being ripped down my thighs, and I realized that I was totally, resoundingly fucked…

"Hey, who the fuck is–"

There was the sound of scuffling shoes, and a hard blow. The other thug went down, crumpling into some boxes. I felt the guy holding me down release his grip and take a step back.

"Who the *fuck* do you think you are?" He snarled. I ripped at the knot of my blindfold, desperate to free myself and see what was really happening.

Whatever was going on, it was a brawl. Fists flew, shoes scraped against the uneven pavement, and grunts of pain were exchanged.

I finally tugged the blindfold free, just in time to watch Lex Lambert dig his knee into the gut of my would-be rapist, dropping him to his knees and palms. Lex paused to check me, and I saw someone rise up behind him – the other asshole, by the looks of it.

With the gag in my mouth, I couldn't shout at the danger or untie my own wrists, so I bobbed my head. Lex turned, just in time to take a walloping blow to the side of his cheek. He slipped, steadying himself against the wall, before bouncing free and headbutting the guy in the nose.

"God*dammit!*" The thug screeched. "By dose!" Blood was gushing from his nose, which was unnaturally bent and partially flattened. "You broke by dose, you fucking biece of shit!"

"I'll break more of you if you touch this fucking woman again," Lex snarled, digging the heel of his boot into the guy's balls.

Whimpering, he clutched himself and collapsed down to his knees. Lex lifted his foot and delivered another kick, this time straight to the side of the guy's head.

"That'll teach ya," he muttered to himself.

He whirled back around and untied the restraints on my wrists. Finally, I managed to tug the gag from my lips, gasping in fear and breathlessness. "Holy shit," I exclaimed. "Holy fucking shit, oh fuck, oh god…"

"It's okay now," Lex whispered, drawing me close. His toughened fingers held my cheeks, and he gazed deeply into my eyes. "I'm here now. They won't hurt you. I've taken care of them…"

The one of the ground had risen up again, and loomed menacingly behind Lex. He was ready to end this, once and for all…

"Lex, *wait!*" I fearfully gasped, staring over his shoulder at the attacker.

He turned, but it was too late. Lex took another solid blow to the head that sent him clattering against the wall, where his head collided with a sick thud. My rescuer crumped to the pavement uselessly, knocked completely out cold.

In that instant, my fingers graced a glass bottle. Before the thug could turn his attention to me, I snatched it up, smashing it upside his head. He took a step back in surprise as I lunged forward with the broken glass, but his foot caught, and he slipped backwards, smashing into a dumpster.

He had just started to get up when I saw it. The gun they'd held on me sat at my feet. I swept it up into my hand, pointing it at the asshole and screaming for him to stay on the ground. Bending over, I shook Lex by his blazer, smacking his face with my free hand. He was out cold, but blood was pooling from his head.

Oh fuck. Oh god, no...

"HELP! " I screamed at the top of my lungs, clutching desperately to any semblance of hope. "CAN ANYBODY PLEASE HELP ME?!"

Chapter 6

Lex

Being a world-class football player meant that waking up in a hospital bed was not *exactly* a foreign experience to me. I'd taken my fair share of blows during the sport, on *and* off the field...

The first thing I noticed was that I was disoriented by the amount of space I had. The kind of treatment I was used to in England would have been cramped at best. Hospitals in London aren't known for their open floorplans.

Here... I had space.

The room was fairly large by my standards, although the huge bed took up a substantial portion of it... but I had it all to myself.

A small television was mounted up on the opposing wall, and there was a wide window to my right, letting in some light to chirp up the place. To my left was a door, leading to either a closet or a bathroom – and beyond that, a larger door, naturally to exit the room.

That's when I spotted the other human being in the room. Riley was fast asleep, curled up on some sort of padded storage bench beneath the window. As I shifted around in bed and found a way to raise the incline to my back, she stirred from her slumber.

"Oh! Lex! You're... you're awake," Riley murmured, stifling her surprising burst of enthusiasm with a yawn. "How are you feeling?"

"My head's a little off, but besides that, I'm chipper as ever," I groggily answered, scratching my chest. I felt round things attached to my skin, connected to wires – so, the doctors had given me electrodes.

"You won't want to mess with those," Riley warned, her eyes drifting down to my scratching fingertips. "They were rather adamant about that."

"*They* being *who*, exactly?"

"The doctors," Riley told me.

"Right. Speaking of, what am I doing in a hospital, precisely?"

Riley looked saddened. "You... took a few blows to the head, and you were knocked out." Her eyes glanced down to her lap, where she wrung her hands together while adding: "There was a lot of bleeding."

"For a head wound? Not surprising at all," I commented, feeling for the lightly throbbing gash on my scalp. My fingertips grazed it – not too bad, all things considered. "I've taken a few before. They always look far worse than they actually are. Lots of blood with those buggers. Scares the Devil right out of you."

"Well… we'd better wait to see what the doctor says, anyway."

I nodded absentmindedly, considering those words. "Where is the doctor, anyway?"

"He's supposed to be making his rounds in thirty minutes," Riley responded, rising from the bench, "but I'll go check with the nurse's station anyway. You've been out for a while, so we didn't know when you might come back."

"How long's *a while?*"

"A day and a half."

I grimaced. "Oh boy."

Riley stepped out, and I reached over, digging around the items scattered across the end table for my phone. I didn't see it, which concerned me – particularly since I knew that Jess was going to be *pissed.*

I spotted my blazer, hanging with my pants on a nearby wall. Shrugging off the blankets, I was able to barely reach it with my electrodes in place, and fished around in my blazer pocket.

There you are...

I slunk back into bed and began to text Jess. My eyes fell upon the logo for the hospital, which had the words "Saint Peter's General Hospital" emblazoned around the edges, and notified her where I was, and that I was fine.

I hit *send* and slipped the phone back onto the end table before Riley popped back into the room.

"Doctor Wright will be with you shortly."

Shortly apparently meant *later than originally told,* because it was almost forty-five minutes before he finally appeared. A comforting man in his mid-thirties, Doctor Wright apologized for the delay and began to examine me during some small talk.

I kept my answers brief, and my tone even.

"Everything *seems* normal," he commented finally, wrapping up his investigation. "Looks like you lucked out. Minor concussion, and you've got that gash there, but I don't see why it won't heal up nicely. You don't even need stitches for it. I'm going to go ahead and clear you for release. Shall I go ahead and file for the paperwork?"

"Please do so," I agreed.

He left us to our devices, and I turned to Riley. "How long have you been here?"

"Since you saved me."

"Saved you?" I didn't remember much saving.

"The… rapists, in the alley," she cautiously reminded me. "I was going to be assaulted and probably left for dead, but you found me… you came for me, and you rescued me from them."

I faintly remembered something like that, but it was incredibly faint. *Did I?* I flexed my knuckles, feeling them ache. It was the kind of ache from battering them against the skulls of predatory, low-life scum.

"Are you okay?" I asked her.

Riley smiled softly. It was maybe the first genuine, sincere smile that I'd seen out of her. "Yeah. I think I'm pretty great."

"Fantastic to hear, love," I smiled back.

"Listen… how long are you going to be in America?" Riley asked me, hovering near the edge of my bed. She looked pensive, tentatively awaiting my answer.

"You know, I'm not quite sure… weeks, probably. I can't stay too long, the season starts back up in a month and a half… and I'm going to have to keep in shape, regardless of where I am."

"Oh. I see." She looked crestfallen.

"Listen, a month and a half, that's a long time, right?" I replied, sensing her withdraw back into herself. *Dammit, it took this long to get her to retreat out of that shell… the last thing I need is to lose her now.*

"Well, not really, when you think about it," Riley told me. "I'd actually say that it's not a whole lot of time at all."

"I want to see more of you," I blurted out, surprised by myself. Riley was apparently startled as well, as she looked at me curiously and with a rather analytical gaze.

"Do you?"

"Yeah," I reiterated. "Only if you think you can handle it."

"I can handle myself," she retorted, "with the notable exception of last night. Call that the exception that proves the rule."

"You know... I like you," I confessed. "The other night was fantastic, and I hope to experience more of those... And less nights that end in a hospital bed..."

Riley hesitated, looking at me with a clear conflict of emotions in her head. Finally, she looked me in the eyes with a startlingly vulnerable gaze, and she spoke: "...Yeah." Adding a nod, she continued: "I think I'd like that."

I nodded back, letting a small grin curve up the corners of my lips. "I think I'd like that too."

The door popped open not five seconds later, and a very flustered Jess was upon me like wildfire.

"Lex, what the *fuck?* Can I not leave you alone for *fookin'* five goddamn minutes without you disappearing on me? And this time... this time, you're in the *hospital?*"

"It was for a worthy cause," I replied, taking Riley's hand. Her fingers flinched, but she kept her hand in mine.

Jess glanced back and forth between us. "So... are one of you going to start talking about why my friend is in a hospital bed right now, or am I going to have to threaten to beat him halfway to death with a brick to get answers?"

"Riley was cornered by a spot of trouble," I answered simply. "I took care of it. Might have gotten a few scrapes in the process."

"He's being modest," Riley elaborated.

"Am I... am I hearing that right?" Jess laughed as she turned back to me, almost in hysterics. "Modest? *You?* Do you even know *how* to be modest? You couldn't even find it in a dictionary, yeah?"

"I was dragged into an alley," Riley told her with complete conviction. "There were two of them, and I couldn't fight them off. Lex found me and fought them off. If he'd been fifteen seconds later…"

Jess went completely silent, staring at me. She looked a very compelling mixture of shocked, appalled, and downright horrified.

"Lex… is this… is this *true*?"

"More or less," I shrugged.

"*Cor blimey,*" she muttered, holding her head in her hand. "I'm gonna need a stiff pint after hearing *that*…" She turned to Riley again, looking at her as if for the first time.

I had to remind myself that, besides a fleeting occasion, it *was* the first time.

"You look like hell," Jess finally told her. "You look like you haven't had a good night's sleep in… a day? Two? What, have you been *here* the entire time?"

Riley nodded. "Yeah."

"What? Why?"

"Because I didn't know how to reach you, I don't know where he's staying, and I didn't think he had anyone else nearby who could care for him. Besides… he'd just saved my life."

Jess tried to hide it, but I could see how she beamed. She couldn't resist making quick, fleeting eye contact with me.

"Listen, I know that it's been a rough couple of days for you… Riley," she started. "But I thought my only friend in this country was laying dead in a ditch somewhere. If it's not too much, can I have a couple of minutes alone with him?"

Riley turned to me. I halfway expected her to be indignant, but she looked somewhat relieved. "I could use a bathroom and some coffee. Do you need anything from out there?"

"I think I'm good."

"Alright. I'll be back in ten."

She nodded cordially to Jess as she left us in the room alone. As soon as the door clicked, I tossed the bedding off and made my way towards the connected bathroom.

"This is perfect," Jess commented over the sound of my filled bladder of piss hitting water. "She adores you now. Not hard to see why."

"Why do you sound so pleased with yourself?" I asked warily, washing my hands in the sink.

"You saved her life, Lex. This is *exactly* the kind of publicity we need you to have. I'm already writing the bylines now… maybe I can whip up something to send over to the boys tonight…"

I popped the door open and began walking uneasily back across the room to my clothes. "Absolutely not."

Jess reacted as if she were a behaving child, and I'd just ripped her favourite toy from her and slipped it well out of reach. "But why not? Surely there's a police report or something, I don't even really need to ask her anything else. She just told me everything I needed to know to finish your write-up…"

"You're not exploiting what happened to her in order to make me look better," I explained sternly.

"But *nothing* happened, thanks to your timely and heroic intervention," Jess protested. "And besides, where the fuck is *this* Lex coming from? Used to be that you'd take *anything* that made you look better."

"I don't follow," I replied, slipping some of my possessions into my blazer and slacks pockets.

"The Patrovo Corporation contract, you *ruddy* idiot," Jess hissed. She nodded towards the door. "You *need* shit like this to make you look better in their eyes. Has Alistair Pritch ever saved anyone from rape? Who knows! But now *Lightning Lex Lambert* has! All of a sudden, you're right at the top of the pile, where we both know you deserve to be."

"Not like this," I reprimanded her. "Absolutely *not* like this. I forbid it."

"You *forbid* it?"

"I do," I snarled, stepping closer to her. "You are not to exploit this woman to further your agenda of representing me."

"For God's sake, exploiting her is why I told you to go find her again! You *pay me* to do this," Jess retorted. "The agenda feeds me. *That* agenda. The agenda that *keeps the British public pleased with you.* Did you forget that you're a loose cannon? You *need* me to pick up after you, Lex! Without me *doing my job*, you'd never get that sponsorship in your wildest dreams!"

"I am not telling you to not do your job," I hissed, practically dribbling acid around my lips. "I am telling you that you leave Riley Ricketts out of it. Are we clear?"

"You've got it bad for this one, don't you?" Jess asked. I could see some revelation unfolding in her eyes.

"I'm not letting anyone – you included – take this traumatic thing she's experienced and force her to live it publicly, going through it again and again," I told her. "It's not the right thing to do."

Jess shook her head. "She's gotten into your brain, man. You *never* troubled yourself with what the *right* thing to do would be. You're changing."

"So what if I am?" I demanded.

"I'm not saying you're changing for the *worse*, Lex," Jess clarified, her tone softening as she looked into my eyes. "I'm saying that it's for the *better*. Whatever you two have, whatever you're doing... you need to capitalize on this."

"You're not exploiting–"

"Not me, *you*," she told me. "Don't you *dare* let this one slip away from you, Lex. You need her. She's going to show you how to be better than who you are… and even when this thing between you both ends, you'll come away from it a stronger, greater man for it."

I thought on this as we heard a knock at the door. Jess mouthed the words, "Think about it," and then walked over and let Riley back into the room.

"Oh, you're… up," Riley commented.

"I think it's time we get out of here, don't you think?" I flashed her a smile. "We could both use a clean, soft place to sleep."

"That sounds good," Riley nodded.

Jess suddenly realized that she was the third wheel, and clasped her hands together. "Well. I think that I've taken up enough of your time now… it's good to see that you haven't dropped dead somewhere," she laughed nervously. Her eyes darted back and forth between the two of us, and she took herself a deep breath.

"Jess, calm down," I commanded her lightly. "You've been itching to see more of New Orleans. Take a guided tour! Hit some pubs, yeah? Get your tourist bullshit out of the way."

I walked over to the tired American woman, placing the backs of my knuckles against her cheek. "I think my friend here can keep me out of trouble from now on... wouldn't you agree, Riley?"

Riley afforded me a small smile.

"Yeah, I think I can probably manage that."

"So it's settled, then," I turned back to my secret publicist. With a mystical wave of my fingers, I let my voice boom: "*I hereby release you, Jessica Partridge, of your bindings. From this moment forth until your services are needed once more, you are free to wander the port of New Orleans, out from under my oppressive reign.*"

Jess did a slow twirl and lifted her fingertips, pretending to rise out from a spell. "*It's over!*" She chortled. "Your evil magic is *gone!* Now, I'm free! Free to not incessantly worry about your constant stream of *bullshit!*"

Jess and I shared a heavy laugh.

Even Riley looked cheerful.

Chapter 7

Riley

Upwards of an hour later, streetcar ride and all, I was leading Lex Lambert up to my apartment. It didn't occur to me until I was unlocking the door that he hadn't seen it... and that we'd been in his hotel room for last time.

This time was going to be a little different.

Lex didn't get the apartment tour. What he *did* get, however, was shown my bedroom, where I pushed him down onto the side of my queen-sized bed.

"You're feeling a bit frisky, aren't you?" Lex muttered huskily, clearly already knowing where this was going.

"Shut up," I told him as I sank to my knees in front of him.

"You're moving rather quickly today–"

I paused, glaring up at him.

"Lex, let me ask you something: do you want your cock in my mouth, or not?"

He instantly shut up.

"That's a good boy."

I ripped at his slacks, unzipping the fabric and helping him kick off his shoes and remove his socks again. He shifted his hips so that I could tug the pants down, leaving him in his boxers, his button-up shirt, tie, and blazer.

"That just looks goofy. Get up."

"I – what?"

"Get up, take everything off, and sit back down again," I commanded. "Or else I'll just shred all of that stuff off of you, and it looks a little on the expensive side…"

Lex took the hint, standing up to disrobe out of his clothes. Everything wound up over the back of my chair, and he was soon relaxing backwards in bed as I crept between his thighs.

His cock looked even bigger in the light. My hand was positively tiny by comparison, but I wrapped my fingers around it, squeezing lightly before giving it a few good strokes.

Already, a bead of precum was forming a pearlescent droplet at the tip of his crown. Eagerly unwilling to waste the gift, I pressed the tip of my tongue against his head, licking the salty bead from the engorged head.

Between that and beginning to stroke him with gusto, Lex leaned his head back into my pillows, groaning with satisfaction.

Before he could grow bored with this, I shifted my fist further down his cock and enveloped the head with my lips. I was unwilling to test how much of him I could take inside just yet, but I wanted to feel his cum spurt out across my tongue, filling my mouth… and I knew that I could definitely get him off to do it.

"Riley…" Lex groaned, clenching one eye as he glanced down at me. With my fingertips, I threaded some strands of hair behind my ear, descending further down his cock with my mouth. "Seeing that just makes me even harder," he continued to groan.

I believed it, feeling how rigid he was inside my mouth. My tongue lapped away around his cock as I took in his essence, eagerly worshipping his thick, juicy erection with my lips, my tongue, my breath… every part of me wanted to please this rugged man who had protected and saved me.

My lips descended faster now, and I found myself rolling into a rhythm as I flicked my tongue along beneath the crest of his head. I felt him groan once more, eager for more of my mouth. His hands pressed down onto my head, fingers intertwining into my locks and wrapping around my scalp.

I obliged him, diving a little deeper, swallowing down more of Lex's cock. I placed my trust in him, letting him guide me now, dictating the motions and the tempo by which my lips pressed down around his throbbing member.

To my surprise, he was gentler than expected. I feared that he might try to force me to take much more of him inside than I could handle, but that wasn't the case at all. He respected my limits – pushing me closer towards them, but never overstepping.

It only made me want to please him more.

My first continued rolling down the length of his slickened erection as I pumped my lips down the rock-hard weapon, purely at the behest of his hands upon my head. Every inch of my body craved him now, demanding his touch, his pressure, and the sensation of him inside me once more.

He released his hands as I lifted my lips off of his cock, a thin trail of saliva connecting them to the glistening head. Rolling my curled fist over his head to stroke the most sensitive folds, I placed my tongue at the bottom of his shaft and licked my way up, then back down, taking one of his large, bouncing globes into my mouth and sucking.

"Oof," he murmured, letting his head glide backwards into the pillows again. "You're incredible…"

I took the compliment with a small smile, sucking on the other testicle instead now as I continued rolling my cupped palm around the head of his cock.

His hands clenched down into my shoulders, and I knew that he was getting closer to the edge. In response, I quickened my speed, sucking and stroking his magnificent tool until I could sense his body begin to shift and his chest begin to groan.

"I'm about to…"

My hands clasped onto his thighs and dug into the skin, and I took down as much of his cock as I could handle – a little over half. As I lightly rolled my mouth around it, I felt his throbbing tool spasm, and rope after rope of his steaming, salty seed pumped across the back of my throat.

"God… fucking… shit!" He gasped out, his hands claiming my scalp again, holding my head down as his body went rigid with passion.

As the last few drops of cum spurted across my tongue, Lex began to slacken his limbs. He released a great, heavy sigh, relaxing completely into the bed with his cock still between my lips… and a massive smile across his own.

I plucked his cock free from my mouth and swallowed the last traces of his gift. I immediately proceeded to lick his pole clean, polishing the shaft to completion with my tongue.

"That was… absolutely incredible," Lex murmured in drained satisfaction. "You are *brilliant* at that, Riley."

I knelt up from between his legs on the bed and curled up beside his great, naked form, tracing his cut muscles with my fingertips. "Glad you enjoyed yourself. I figured it was the very least that I could–"

He was already slipping down the bed and beside my hips, whipping up the edge of my dress.

"Wait, what are you–"

"I knew it," Lex grinned up at me.

"Knew *what,* exactly?" Although, I knew just what he was talking about.

"You're so wet for me," he smiled, tugging at the thin veneer under my dress and across my soaked pussy. I was still in my clothes from the other night, and that included the thong…

And that very thong was now being tugged down my thighs and dropped to the floor.

Before I could even pretend to protest, he was burrowing his face between my legs, lapping away at my slickened folds. It was my turn to thread my fingers through his thick hair, tugging him down into my sex and gasping at the touch of his tongue.

"Oh, Lex… *fuck…*"

His tongue began to tease my clit, flicking the engorged bead of my passion. My hips lifted in response, but he kept me pinned down to the bed, his great strength trapping me right where he wanted me.

With a light sucking motion, he slipped it partially into his mouth, rolling it over his tongue and nuzzling his face against my folds. It was all I could do to keep myself from screaming with pleasure.

Good fucking god, he's good at this, I thought to myself. *Holy shit, how did I ever think I could turn down more of THIS?*

I felt the tip of a finger part my wet chasm, and a second joined it shortly after. He pressed his digits inside, curling them to manipulate the small bundle of nerves inside. Meanwhile, his mouth released my clit, the tongue tracing the hood and teasing along the very edges, unwilling to drive me too far into total sensitivity.

It was just the way that I loved it.

Lex continued to play my sex like an instrument, his mouth deftly working my body with gusto. I realized how deeply into his scalp I was digging my fingertips, but I couldn't fathom the thought of releasing even an ounce of pressure.

At the same time, my thighs opened and closed unexpectedly; sometimes, they slackened as I enjoyed his expert touch... but other times, they squeezed tight, trapping his skull in a vice between my legs.

His fingers, stained with my juices, finally plucked free from my chasm. Lex paused to lick them lightly before reaching up to caress my face, and I took his hand and dove them into my mouth. Cleaning the fluids off with my tongue, I murmured out another moan of satisfaction before releasing his hand.

It returned down below, and he shouldered my thighs and clenched his fingertips down into the supple skin, holding them tightly around his head as he absolutely went for it.

As Lex married his mouth to my lower lips, his tongue darted along my clit in unpredictable but jaw-dropping patterns, forcing my body to react with a twitching spine and writhing hips. As he held me close, I kept him there, pressing down harder on his head as my hips rose to meet his pressure.

"Oh god, just like that," I murmured. "Don't stop. Just keep doing that… oh god… oh *Lex*… oh fuck me, I'm… I'm…"

My syllables descended into incoherent babbling, followed by sharp, loud moaning, and then a stifled scream. I felt pleasure whiplash down my spine as the forceful string of orgasms came, rocking my body and leaving me in complete, blinding bliss.

I'd experienced complete sexual fulfillment before. Less often that I'd liked with my partners, but a lucky few choices had brought me to that edge and pushed me all the way.

But when Lex did it…

This was completely different.

I felt a total alignment of ecstasy across my body. Every nerve ending burst into paradise as my body quivered with relentless, bursting satisfaction… I had been driven up to the highest precipice of pleasure, and then sent careening wildly down into a pit of wanton, carnal bliss.

It was only after the succession of multiple climaxes finally ended that I realized how hard my thighs had clamped around his head. As I released my vice grip on his head, feeling my entire body trembling with ache, I collapsed down into the bed and let my breasts heave with complete orgasmic release.

"How," I murmured. "How was that even better than last time?"

Lex pulled up beside me in bed, supporting his head with a planted elbow in the pillows. "The last time was just a little fun together, but now we trust and respect one another."

"Do we?" I asked, not meaning to antagonize, but merely requesting clarification.

"I certainly like to think so, love," he chuckled in that smooth British accent.

My eyes fell upon his skull, and I remembered the blow he'd taken to it... and the resultant gash. "Oh god. Lex! I'm so sorry! I completely forgot about–"

"It's perfectly okay," he smiled handsomely. "I'd have indicated something if you'd been hurting me. They gave me some mild painkillers for it, and I didn't notice any pain–"

He stopped, groaning for a moment before sinking into the pillows.

"Oh, dammit, I should have known better than to fuck you straight out of the hospital," I bitterly told myself, leaning up to check out his wound. "At least it's not bleeding…"

"I'll be fine," Lex mumbled. "I just need to take it a little easy for a moment. Believe me, I'm not feeling any pain…"

"Is that so?" I asked quietly, tracing his muscles with my fingertips again.

"Yeah, I believe so. That adrenaline, those chemicals in my head… gotta love those endorphins. They make for great therapy."

"Well, if that's so," I smiled, clutching onto his thick cock. To my amazement, he was still mostly hard, with just the slightest limpness to it. I knew how to clear *that* up, though.

I began to stroke his cock again, feeling it gradually stir back to full power within my hand.

"What, *again?* You're going to spoil me," Lex chuckled, starting to lean up.

"No, no," I insisted, pressing him back down with my free palm against his pectoral. "You just lay back and let me do all the work, okay? Let me take care of you... the best way I know how to right this moment."

Lex smiled softly.

"I guess I can't argue with that..."

As his cock thrummed with power, I slowly lifted an ankle, shifting myself into a straddle over him. But it was more convenient with the angle to face away from him, and I thought he might appreciate the view of my ass, bouncing up and down his massive cock...

Slowly lowering my wet, fulfilled lips down around his crimson head, I gasped at how it stretched me. As I held his cock upright with one graceful hand, I gradually sank my hips down his wet erection, inching my way down until I was finally hilting him again.

"Gotta say, I quite enjoy this view..."

"Knew ya would," I smiled over my shoulder, biting my bottom lip. "Now, like I said, just relax and let me take care of you..."

Slipping one hand into my hair to hold it up and tug against a handful of follicles, I slipped the other against one of his thighs for support. While my hips began to rock against his, I felt his hands slide around them, the fingers clenching in as he started meeting my motions with the sturdy, powerful swaying of his pelvis…

Chapter 8

Lex

The convenience of being on vacation in the States and sleeping with a self-employed painter was that we got to see a whole lot of each other as the weeks dragged on by.

My scrapes from the alleyway incident cleared up rather quickly, and I was back to my usual, robust self. This presented me with certain responsibilities that it became time to resume.

Although hours of practically daily sex made for excellent exercise, I made sure to return to my proper training regiment. A nearby gym accepted me for a month's contract, and I began making good use of the weights, the track, and the indoor swimming pool.

Meanwhile, I didn't see a lot of Jess. We kept in touch via text messaging, checking in with each other every day. She grew highly attached to the landmark New Orleans streetcars, eagerly riding down the Garden District through St. Charles Street, or hopping onto the other lines and experiencing the downtown views.

I, on the other hand, grew highly attached to my company here in New Orleans. When I expressed an interest in seeing some of the historical spots as well, Riley took it upon herself to arrange some tours.

We spent about half a week inseparable from one another; she took me to see the National World War II Museum, the Audubon Aquarium and Zoo of the Americas, the St. Louis Cathedral and Cemetery, the Jean Lafitte National Park (where we enjoyed boat tours and wetlands trips), the cultural Frenchman Street and Jackson Square, and much more.

At least now I had something meaningful to chat with Jess about, other than *Yeah, fucking my American girl is still fun as hell.*

We took a taxi across the Lake Pontchartrain Bridge towards Covington – the largest bridge over water in the world. The city on the other side was sprawling and sparse, and I soon directed us back across to see the magnificently large lake again. It was easy to imagine that I was actually crossing an ocean, as the distant shorelines receded out of sight.

At my behest, Riley took me to see some of the museums in town as well. Although she was far more hesitant about that particular prospect, I insisted on it – and on her promising that we would visit galleries that held her art.

"Are you sure?" She asked tentatively as we stood outside a nondescript building, wedged tightly between the others. A modest sign jutted from the bricks – *Valliere Museum of Art.*

"Positive," I smiled radiantly.

"Well… okay," she conceded, taking a deep breath. "Come on in, then."

I followed her up the steps and stepped through the doors. As soon as we were inside, the atmosphere *instantly* changed – the museum was contemporary, playing soft, upbeat chillstep as the otherwise dim rooms flowed with splashes of blue lighting.

"This is beautiful," I commented warmly. "Are *all* American museums like this?"

"Like what?" She asked thoughtfully.

"So unassuming on the *outside*, but so magnificently full of life and culture on the *inside*," I remarked in response. "I can't say I remember the last time I've been in a museum, but I understand most of the ones back home to be rather... stuffy. Stuffy and drab."

"That would make sense," Riley replied. "England is much older, naturally. I imagine that the vast majority of the museums there have been historic, cultural staples for many, many decades... perhaps centuries, a lot of them. Things that old tend to be fairly resilient to change."

"I would expect an institute such as a museum to adapt to the times, perhaps," I retorted as we took in a room full of vases and ancient tools.

"You might think that, but there's a certain prestige and elegance to the traditional method of representing things," she told me. "Sometimes, the old ways are better."

After thirty minutes of strolling from exhibit to exhibit, we finally came across a small room, filled with at least a dozen paintings. The styles clashed a bit, including artwork reflective more of older art styles, paired with contemporary landscapes, and several portraits of animals in various painting modes.

"Well, here we are," Riley chuckled nervously.

"These are *yours?*" I asked, stepping forward to admire the work.

"They are."

I glanced around the room, taking in the various pieces. Although there were a couple that seemed like rather... *interesting* choices, the vast majority of the paintings were crafted with such talent and care that it took my breath away.

"These are fantastic, Riley," I whispered to her, trying to keep from gushing.

Of course, she had *told* me herself that she was a talented painter with artwork featured in various museums around the country, but a part of me reserved interest for actually seeing this with my own eyes.

My gaze fell upon a small sign near the doorway, featuring her headshot and a short biography.

It was unmistakably her.

Riley Ricketts.

"You… don't need to read that," she quickly tugged me away, her arm looped through mine. "Anyway, you've seen my art now. Satisfied?"

"The other museums, do they carry different paintings than these?"

"I sell them my originals," she responded. "Some of them have taken it upon themselves to license reproductions, but yes, virtually all of the museums here in town that carry me have different selections of my work."

"Can I see more?" I asked.

"You… really want to?" She seemed surprised, and I couldn't imagine why.

"Of *course* I do, Riley," I told her. "This part of your life is one you haven't shared with me yet, and I want to see more of it… but only if you're comfortable with the prospect."

An approaching young man interrupted us. He was dressed immaculately with his hair tucked behind his ears, a pair of thick glasses over his eyes, and feminine charm in everything from his strut to his facial features.

"Oh, dear me, it's really you, isn't it?"

Riley stiffened up slightly, but put a mildly charmed smile on her face. "I assume so, yes."

"Oh, Miss Ricketts, it's an absolute pleasure to meet you," he emphatically told us. "I'm a huge fan of your work. I don't want to bother you for too long... but could you take a selfie with me?"

She blinked a few times, then laughed.

"You... want to take a picture."

"Of course! If that's not too much trouble, that is. My friends and I, we've followed your skill for some time. My older brother bought one of your paintings a decade ago, long before all this!"

He nervously chuckled, throwing his arms up to indicate the room. "Not that, I mean, you completely deserve the recognition, I wasn't saying—"

"Your brother," Riley commented, putting his star-struck stammer to a stop. "Who is he?"

"Jackson Wilcox," he replied with a wide smile. "I think he said you two went to school together a long time ago—"

"Jax? I remember Jax!"

Riley beamed with pleasure. "I think I remember you, too. I recall a younger Wilcox, the one time I was over at his house.. a little rambunctious thing in a Cookie Monster onesie, watching cartoons the entire time. Was that you?"

"Guilty as charged. I used to love that thing."

Riley chuckled, moving into position next to him. "Alright, then. One selfie. Let's do it."

He smiled like a goofball, then whipped out his phone and flicked to the camera app. Holding it outstretched in front of them on portrait mode, he threw up a thumbs up with his free hand as she slipped her arm around him and summoned up a smile.

I was used to this treatment, but I hadn't realized that she was this popular here. Sure, it wasn't quite the levels of a World Cup football star… but there was an incredible validation in a stranger off the street, recognizing your skills, and wanting to freeze forever in time the moment that they bumped into you.

My willingness to pose with fans had really worked in my favour, although

I'd always been fine with it. It was less an *ego* thing, and much more a *flattery* thing.

Well… maybe it was an *ego* thing anyway.

After it was done, they examined the picture together. "Not too bad," she observed. "Anyway, I'm about to get going, but it's nice to bump into you after all this time. Tell Jax I said 'Hi' the next time you see him… and that I'm still the better arm wrestler."

"Will do!" He grinned, before looking from her to me, and then back to her again. "Listen, Riley… if you're not doing anything tonight…"

"I'm busy," she robotically answered, "but flattered."

"Right," he quickly chuckled through the rejection, suddenly aware that I wasn't alone. "Right… well… it was great to see you again. You take care now, alright?"

"Will do," she nodded. "You too."

We took our leave of the museum. "That's the chirpiest I think I've seen you yet," I commented to her.

"Yeah, that was exhausting," she confided. "It's rare that I bump into a fan, but it usually drains me to keep up the cheeriness for more than a couple of seconds."

"Is that so?" I asked.

"Definitely. I don't have the energy for that. It's a part of the reason why I keep to myself… the longer I'm on the streets, the more that people recognize me."

"You aren't flattered?"

"I don't need the flattery."

I shrugged. "Should we skip the other museums? If you're worried about bumping into other fans…"

"Could we, just for today?" She pleaded. "I wasn't going to ask, but if you're offering…" She saw my expression change, and quickly rectified her tone: "I will *absolutely* take you on other days, but that was one of the smaller museums… I don't think I want to deal with that too much more for today…"

"Absolutely," I embraced her with one arm, leading her away from the museum. "I don't see a problem with that at all… and if you'd like, just tell me some of the other galleries, and I'll go visit them independently of you."

Riley looked up at me with an impish grin. "We'll see," she replied, right before pecking her lips against my cheek.

We were feeling kind of hungry, and her Japanese friend ran a sandwich shop, so we put two and two together. Luckily, *Witch Wiches* wasn't further away than a fifteen-minute taxi ride, and we strolled through the doors during its slow period.

"No, no, *no!* What is the *matter* with you?!"

One of the teenagers behind the counter glanced up stupidly from a meat-slicing machine, which was making a vicious scraping noise. The Japanese friend of Riley's – *Reiko*, I think I'd been told – was making an absolute fuss over the disaster.

"I don't know what happened," the kid dumbly told her. "I put it on the right settings. This stupid thing is a broken piece of junk."

Reiko glowered at him. "This *stupid thing* is a *three thousand dollar* piece of equipment that works *fine*.

Parker, *you* are the piece of junk. Get the hell out of the way so that I can fix this freaking thing… *again*…"

She fiddled with the settings as we approached the counter, and he vacantly gazed over our way. "Oh, you've got it on the *fourth setting… and* you've turned it up to *high?* No freaking wonder it's on the fritz… how you figured out how to damage an analog slicing machine, I have *zero* freaking clue…"

He started to take our orders, ignoring my requests for recommendations, when Reiko poked her head up and glanced over.

"Oh! Riley! And Handsome English Dude! Why didn't you tell me you were coming by?"

"It was a last-second thing," I smiled. "How are you? Kid's got you bothered?"

Her face fell as she tilted her head. "Boy, you have *no* freaking idea how much of a snot-nosed little brat these teenagers can be on an individual basis... slap a crew of them together, and I'm constantly putting out fires."

"Fire?" The kid asked, perking up.

"No, you insane pyromaniac," she told him. "Don't you *dare* think about fire. You just get over there and start making sandwiches, or the closest *fire* you'll find is a freaking pink slip."

He wandered over to the side, and she started giving out glowing recommendations of some of the offerings at her dine-in. Within ten minutes, we were eating some of the most delicious sandwiches that I'd ever tasted – completely complimentary.

"That's not half bad," I told her when she swung by to check on us, pulling up a barstool to our high-top table.

"Oh yeah?" She grinned, nodding along. "You *like* that fried alligator sub, don't'cha?"

"It's pretty damned delicious," I agreed.

"One of my favorites," Reiko replied, then jabbed a thumb Riley's way. "Can never get this one to try any of the cool stuff…"

"I like the traditional ones," she answered defensively. "Nothing's wrong with a chicken cordon bleu."

"But that's so *uninspired.* Chicken and ham, dude! What's exciting about *that?* Try out the wacky shit sometime!" Her voice went sing-song as she continued. "I can guarantee that you'd liiiike iiiit…"

"When's the last time I've enjoyed a recommendation of yours?"

She looked between the two of us. "Um. Remember that one time that I convinced you to come downstairs and head to the bar with me? When I mentioned the *totally hot British guy, sipping away at his–*"

"*Point taken,*" Riley quickly interjected. "Point very, *very* taken."

"Oh?" I chuckled between bites. "*That* sounds like a story."

"Don't you dare," she cut in, glaring daggers at Reiko. Well… very dull, half-joking daggers, but daggers nevertheless.

"Try something cool next time, and I won't!"

"*Fine.*"

"Fine, what?" Reiko smiled widely.

"Fine, I *promise* to try something 'cool' next time," Riley answered in defeat.

"See! I don't really ask for much, do I?" She laughed, aiming the question mostly my way. "It's all bellyaching with this one. Total stick in the mud. Set in her ways... sometimes, you've just gotta break her out of that shell, you know?"

"I think I'm starting to see that," I grinned.

Riley looked between both of us.

"I don't think I like you two being friends."

"Oh, c'mon bruh!" Reiko laughed again, throwing an arm around my shoulder. "Inseparable as *fuck*. We're two peas in a pod! Two beans on a stalk! Two..."

The scraping noise started up again, and she almost lost her shit completely.

"God*dammit, Parker*!"

When she leapt off the barstool and went to go rescue her expensive restaurant equipment from her crewmember again, Riley and I shared an eye roll as we tore back into our sandwiches.

I realized in that moment that just I couldn't ignore it anymore. This girl was absolutely wonderful, and I deeply enjoyed our time together…

…And I thought that I might just love her.

Chapter 9

Riley

The next time I lifted a paintbrush, I was astonished at how quickly I slipped into the zone. The colors came naturally to me, and the delicate, intricate swiping of bristles against canvas sang a chorus of victory into my ears.

A few hours later, I was facing another landscape painting. To the untrained eye, it was just like my previous, failed paintings – dozens of them, sitting in the Closet of Doom in my apartment.

But this painting didn't belong there.

I gazed at the soft strokes of paint, at how the creek raced down the forest floor. It hooked a steady bend in the foreground, pouring down a steep, brief drop-off into a bed of smoothed large stones. The water turned white with activity, rustling towards the viewer, carving its path through the trees.

There was no other life here, no traces of animals nipping at the rushing water or tucked away behind the flora. It was only a glimpse into the woods, flowing with berry bushes, strong and sturdy trees, and sprawling branches.

All of which gave way for their passionate, reigning god: the roaring, rustling creek, choosing its own place and cutting a path of life through the rest.

I smiled to myself: *the magic is back.*

I began to clean up, washing my brushes and checking the easel to ensure the paint would dry to an optimum efficiency. The last thing I needed was for my first acceptable painting in months to fuck up in the cool-down process.

For the first time that day, I thought about Connor and Reiko. They had both grown busy with their prospective jobs, and I'd been filling my time with Lex…

But Connor in particular was starting to become somewhat of a hassle.

It had been obvious since high school that he was developing feelings for me. The advent of college, and even disappearing for a year off to Finland, had done nothing to push those feelings down… and now that we were growing into our mid-twenties, he was finding it hard to keep himself restrained.

He thought, perhaps, that he was being sly with the obvious glances, the lingering gaze, and the way he'd drop whatever he was doing to come drag around me if opportunity struck. The only reason I didn't see more of him than Reiko was that he was kept so busy running his record store.

But as soon as Lex Lambert had entered the picture…

Perhaps it was because Lex was clearly hanging around, and I was clearly fine with it. Maybe it was because Connor knew that I was a total Anglophile, and that dating – or even just *fucking* – a handsome, older British man was too much for him to ignore.

Either way…

He was clearly aggravated about this.

That's why I kept myself occupied a lot of the time. I started to blow him off, when I was really hanging out with Reiko, or sometimes I'd tell the truth and let him know that I was going over to Lex's place, or he was coming to mine.

I thought back to the previous day, when he'd cornered me at my place and invited me out for breakfast. Reiko was busy with the shop, and I didn't have any excuse to not go… and I felt a little bad about constantly blowing him off.

So I had gone out with him.

"There's something wrong with him," Connor confided over a half-eaten stack of pancakes and some bacon slices. "What's he doing, hanging around here anyway?"

"Will…" I muttered. "Don't do this." The conversation had been going so well. We'd been talking about his record business and my paintings, but inevitably…

"Don't do what?" He asked, almost accusingly. "He doesn't have a day job, he lives out of some cheap hotel, he was just sitting and drinking every night until you showed up… he goes and visits around the city, but *why* is he here?"

"I don't know," I shrugged.

"What do you mean, *you don't know?*"

"I mean, I never bothered to really ask him most of those details," I answered defensively. "He's some kind of football player on vacation here. What's to know?"

"He wears high-end suits and disguises how loaded he probably is," Connor stated, remaining on the offensive. "It's suspicious."

"It's pissing me off," I replied.

"You too, huh? I knew you weren't that dense." He grinned, swallowing down another bite. "Let's see what we can dig up on this guy. Have you even googled him?"

"No, Will, *you're* pissing me off," I told him. "Just fucking drop it, okay? If there's something there, he'll tell me, alright? I trust him. I don't need this to get complicated. I *like* that it's something simple… something easy. There's a hard deadline set, and he'll be gone soon. Just let me fucking have this while it's here to be had."

Connor looked positively wounded. "But Riley, I just don't want you to be–"

"To be hurt?" I hissed. "I'll be fine. You've known me for a long time, Will. I've got thicker skin than most. I'll manage."

"Speaking of that…"

I noticed him take a deep breath.

Oh, no. Not now. Don't do this.

"Riley… I tried to keep it to myself, but I can't help it anymore," he began, clearly lowering himself to the point of complete vulnerability in front of my eyes. "I love you. I've always loved you. Ever since we were kids, and I fought off that bully for you–"

"This isn't the time," I insisted.

"When *is* the time, Riley?" He demanded. "It's *never* the right time, is it? Because you don't want to hear it. And that's fine for you and all, but I can't help the way that I feel–"

"Will, please stop," I pressed. "You *know* that I'm with Lex. If you had to let this out *now*, you could have waited another month or so–"

"That's not good enough," he told me under no uncertain terms. "I know that you're falling for him. God, Riley, it's so fucking obvious. And I've seen how he looks at you, too. You're both going to hurt each other, and that's all there is to it.

"And then I'm going to have to come in and scoop you up, just like I always do when you get too attached to a guy."

I paused warningly, raising an eyebrow.

"...Excuse me?"

Connor realized his mistake, but it was too late for him to back out of the corner he'd painted himself into. "Wait... that's not what I meant. Riley, you know that I'll always be there for you–"

"We're finished," I told him, rising up from the seat and tossing down a ten and a five onto the table in front of him. "I'm taking a few days. I'll contact you first. Leave me alone."

I didn't look over my shoulder as I left the restaurant, abandoning him to the rest of his meal alone.

But that was yesterday.

I checked on the painting again. It wasn't just good... It was perfect. I couldn't let Connor get under my skin. Things were going well for the first time in a long time...

After changing into some casual clothes, I heard my ringtone pinging from the living room. Kicking back into a chair, I snatched up my phone and glanced at the caller ID.

It was one of the local galleries, which I considered odd, but they usually only reached out to me if there was a substantially good reason.

"Hello, Miss Ricketts?"

"Adam!" I grinned to myself affably. "How are you, my love?" Of all the others, it was incredibly rare that the Pulliam Museum reached out to me, let alone the head curator. "I hope all is well down there."

"Things are splendid," he responded in his usual, casual tone… although I sensed something just beneath the surface. "In fact, things are a little *better* than splendid… I just received a rather interesting phone call."

"Sounds curious. Do tell."

His voice dropped to a near-whisper. "We are apparently about to host a rather distinguished guest, Ms. Ricketts… I just got off the phone with one *Gloria Van Lark.*"

My heart stopped in my chest.

"Miss Ricketts? Are you there, Miss Ricketts?"

I swallowed the burst of emotion that threatened to surge out of my throat. "I am absolutely, *definitely* here, Adam."

"Good. You are in New Orleans, I trust?"

"I'm at my apartment now, just thirty or forty minutes away."

"Excellent. She was rather particular about an artist's work that she wanted to peruse... and indicated that she had already scoured a few other galleries in the last couple of days. I sincerely think that you should get down here immediately."

Gloria Van Lark was here?

And she was looking at my *work?*

WHY AM I JUST HEARING ABOUT THIS NOW.

"Absolutely. Oh god, Adam, thank you so much for contacting me. I had no idea that she was here!"

"Neither did I, truthfully," he receded back into his typical casual tone. "I have excellent working relationships with the other galleries in town, but it would appear that none of them saw fit to indicate this… *delicate* matter to me. Oh well. She is expected within the hour. It might serve you to represent yourself…"

"I'm heading out the door as we speak," I lied, glancing over towards my closet and already running clothing options through my head.

"See to it that you are, my dear. *Bonne chance, mon amie!*"

"*Merci, monsieur!*"

With that, I haphazardly dove towards the closet, quickly settling on a conservative yet trendy outfit that highlighted a prim, subtle sense of style.

As I locked the door and darted down the stairs towards the streets of New Orleans, I dug out my phone and sent a group text to Reiko and Will.

Yes, even Will.

He was one of the very few people in the world who understood the gravity of what was happening here… and how utterly important this moment was to me.

"Gloria Van Lark is here, and she's prowling the local galleries featuring my art as we speak."

A few minutes later, Reiko responded:

"GET IT, GIRL."

And then Will:

"I knew this day would come :) Good luck!"

Unsurprisingly, he was just happy that I was talking to him again, even if only in passing.

The massive smile stayed glued to my face all the way down to the Pulliam Museum, where I flashed my *Gallery Pass* to the front attendant and strolled into the building.

I wasn't sure what to do with myself, or what kind of signal to expect that would indicate her presence, so I went ahead and walked towards the exhibit that carried some of my signature work.

Ascending up the white tile stairs, I took in the surroundings of the Pulliam Museum. It was a rather modern piece of architectural elegance, built to emphasize light and luminescence.

During the day, the various skylights, glass ceilings, and reflective surfaces shimmered a dazzling but not blinding force of light across the main atrium and aortic passages, emphasizing ample use of vertical space with winding staircases.

At night, however, the sunken lighting took over, enhancing the entire museum with an astounding array of modern brightness that bathed the careful architecture and beautiful tiling work with majesty, grace, and exquisite accent.

It was one of my favourite places in the city, and it was a tremendous honor to have an exhibit dedicated to my paintings. The fact that I'd gained a fantastic working relationship with the head curator, Adam Garmont, was simply a coveted perk.

With some time to spare before her arrival, I ascended the last few stairs before the drop-off to my corner of the gallery. I turned at the passage away from the ascent, striding alongside the circular railing that gave a stunning view of the lower atrium levels, and passed several galleries featuring recovered artifacts and priceless art that made my head spin.

But that was nothing compared to when I stepped into my gallery.

Gloria Van Lark matched every story I heard of her. With her attention focused on a wintery landscape piece I'd painted on a five-foot canvas, she stood tall, hawkish, with long black hair and half-moon spectacles. She was dressed in form-fitting black attire under a flowing coat, a colorful shawl, and a pair of white, cubic earrings that glistened as the light touched the fine jewelry tips.

Oh sweet Jesus, Gloria Van Lark is here.

I could feel my phone buzz in my pocket, and I moved to silence the tone from my group texts. Although she stood thirty feet away, Gloria's head twisted to regard me coolly, and her face settled into a small, wicked smile.

"You should know better than to disturb others with your technology, Riley."

Just hearing her lips speak my name clashed against the incredible embarrassment I felt at the social *faux pas*. I quickly dug my phone out and silenced it, slipping it back into my purse.

"Miss Van Lark, it is... an absolute pleasure to finally meet you," I spoke as I approached her, summoning all the courage my heart could muster.

"Charmed," she spoke almost sarcastically, extending her delicately manicured hand. I noticed a flash of green across her nails as I lightly shook it, matching her pressure.

"What brings you to New Orleans?" I asked politely.

She ignored the question, turning back to face the wintery landscape. "I see that you rely on a clear coat water-based style. Popularized to American culture by the famous Bob Ross."

"I grew up watching his work," I nodded, fondly remembering his thick, curly afro, his soft and gentile voice, and the kindness in those old, warm eyes.

"Yes, as did many," she replied. "He did great things for making the production of passable art accessible to otherwise talentless imbeciles... in some cases, those said imbeciles came to learn a touch of greatness... it was rare, but it happened."

I nodded along, trying to determine if she was commenting on American culture, or insulting me. I assumed it was probably both.

"I've heard of you in passing, Riley."

"What have you heard of me?" I asked, trying to keep the sheer curiosity out of my tone.

"A number of things: that you've a natural at your craft, that you work quickly and efficiently, that you are a humble but confident artist with friendly working relationships with a dozen museums in this city alone... what do you have to say about these things?"

I was caught a little off-guard as she turned her undivided attention to me, the creases around her eyes settling into a deep, analytic gaze.

"I... would say that you haven't heard wrong," I responded. "I work hard at this," I waved to the paintings surrounding us. "I've dedicated my life to the craft. I've been lucky enough to support myself exclusively through my art... sent on international retreats... that I've–"

"Yes, yes, your resume is very impressive," she drolly commented. "If you honestly think I care even the *slightest* about your past, then you fail to grasp what will earn a single spot in the *Spinnoc*."

Her eyes narrowed. "Tell me, Riley, do you *deserve* a place in the *Spinnoc*?"

I didn't know how to answer this, and I suspected that it was a trick question. *Does she want me to be bold, or does she want me to be humble? What does this woman* want *from me?*

I answered the first thing that came to mind.

"...No."

Her eyes flared open.

I clarified: "Miss Van Lark, with absolutely all due respect... I don't *deserve* a spot, but I *want* one. It's all I've wanted for years... and I feel that I can earn it, if I haven't already."

It was only then that I noticed a few other patrons in the gallery, perusing my art. They appeared to recognize me, which wasn't difficult, given that my face was on a nearby wall-mounted foam board with a short biography. It was a few small groups of people: one, a lithe, elderly woman, was speaking to a younger couple in a hushed tone and watching me.

Gloria Van Lark leaned in closely with a crisp, cold smile, so that only I could hear her response: "I will be in touch, Miss Ricketts."

With that, she lifted her chin and strolled from the room, leaving me stone-faced and defeated. I knew what that meant. I'd heard the stories.

The legendary curator had turned me down.

My shoulders rose as I took in a deep, hectic breath, struggling to come to grips with the opportunity that had just sailed past me.

"What a bitch," an old voice whispered quietly to me. I turned my head, snapping back to reality, and noticed the lithe, elderly woman at my side. "Who was that, anyway?"

"Her name is Gloria Van Lark," I answered mechanically, feeling the life start to slip back into my veins. "She's a powerful and influential curator... she headhunts for one of the most prestigious museums in the country."

The old woman chuckled. "She didn't look all that impressive to me. All that black? Bah. What is it with people and black? You're in a museum, not a godforsaken funeral! Chirp up!"

I couldn't help but laugh.

"That's right, that's a good girl," the woman smiled softly. "You're the one who painted all of this, aren't you? What was it… Riley Ricketts?"

"That's me," I nodded. "Do you like it?"

She gave the room another glance. "If you want an old crone's opinion… I certainly think you've got a knack for this. How long have you been painting?"

"Since I was old enough to hold a paintbrush."

"Heh. Good answer. A little cliché, but it gets the point across," she winked. "Anyway… don't get your hopes down. Sounded like you really respected that woman… I'm sure you'll get another chance down the line. You never know. Maybe it's just not your time yet."

I smiled fondly at her. "You're very kind."

"I'm told that sometimes," she laughed. "Well… I've got to get back to my grandson." She indicated the male half of the younger couple, standing over to the side, near the exit of the room. They didn't appear to be watching for her. "But before I go, why don't we look at this one together?"

She pointed me towards one of my earlier pieces, the painting of an arguing couple on a bridge during noon. I had been experimenting with a post-modern influenced style at the time. I wasn't terribly fond of this one anymore, but it was considered a classic in the circles who appreciated my work.

"Why don't you tell me what you were thinking when you painted this one?" She whispered behind me.

I fell into a small trance, thinking back on that time in my life. It was before I had won the Finland scholarship, and taken the artist's retreat. It was from a more chaotic time, when I still struggled with my foster parents and their wishes for the direction I was going to take in life.

I snapped out of my thoughts. "I don't think very much when I paint," I answered. "But this comes from a rough time in my teenage years… at the time, I was conflicted over–"

Glancing back over my shoulder, I noticed that the three of them – elderly museum patron included – were completely gone.

With a soft, recollecting smile, I silently thanked the stranger for her tenderness and her kindnesses, and I turned back to silently regard my old painting once again.

Chapter 10

Lex

I got it into my head that I wanted Riley to see a little more of the kind of lifestyle I usually led. That's why I booked a private suite in one of the most expensive hotels around, surprising her in her apartment with a room pass.

"The Frione?" She asked, tilting her head as she studied the small, plastic card on its lanyard. "You booked us a room at the freaking *Frione*?"

"I did," I chuckled, crossing my arms. "Room is already prepared and everything."

"But that's such an exclusivist hotel," she thought aloud, turning back to face me. "How did you afford that?" Her gaze changed, and she stiffened up a little. "How much money *do* you have, Lex?

"Enough to cover my bases," I answered conservatively, cocking my eyebrow. "Are you coming along, or are you going to just sit there and gawk at that card?"

"Give me half an hour," she replied, dashing towards her bedroom.

I made myself comfortable as I heard her rummage through her room, slapping together a bag of the "essentials." When she eventually came back out, dressed in a sleek dress with a small suitcase, I couldn't help but stare openly at her.

"What's the matter?" Riley asked.

"You… look absolutely beautiful."

For the first time, I watched her blush. "Th-thank you," she murmured, before composing herself and carrying the case straight past me. "You don't look so bad yourself, handsome."

I stood up from her couch, straightening my tailored suit and running my fingers through my thick hair. "Thanks, buttercup," I grinned. "Shall we be off?"

I followed her downstairs and hailed a taxi. Twenty minutes later, we were strolling through the lobby of the lavish Frione hotel, taking in the sights of the beautiful smoked marble and Grecian columns.

One of the delights to this hotel was the glass elevator to the private upper suites. Running up the outside of the building, we were treated to a phenomenal view of Downtown New Orleans as the elevator ascended. Night had just fallen across the port city – the sea of lights and extravagance beneath us stretched in every direction. In the distance, we spotted the pair of parallel Crescent City Connection bridges that crossed the Mississippi River, stretching far and rising high into the sky from the twirling tangle of Interstate highways.

"It's so beautiful up here," Riley purred.

"Only with you here," I whispered in her ear. I could practically sense the light hairs standing up on the back of her neck, and she turned to face me with vulnerable but hungry eyes.

We still had several floors to go, but the view wasn't going anywhere. Our lips locked as I pulled her into my warm embrace, and Riley's wrists dangled together around the back of my neck.

"Oh, Lex," she murmured between kisses. "What did I ever do to deserve you?"

"I was thinking the same thing," I told her.

It was true. My time with her was better than I could have possibly dreamed. When I'd come to America, I'd hoped for a few good lays, keeping my head down and trying some of the local New Orleans flavour…

But none of that mattered now.

Riley Ricketts fulfilled me. She drew my attention and swelled to occupy my every waking thought. The more time we spent together, the less willing I was to part… and I knew, painfully so, that we didn't have more than a few weeks together.

I heard Jess's thoughts in the back of my head.

Find a nice American girl.

Bring her back.

Show Brett Barker you can settle.

Sure, that had been part of the plan… but now my fixation on gaining the sponsorship through playing the part became more intimately involved with a different objective altogether.

I sensed something new and very much alive, curling up from the bottom of my heart like smoke in the dark.

Do I dare admit it to myself?

We parted lips, and I realized how primal our breathing had become. Our chests heaved together as we watched one another, gazing deep and passionately into each other's eyes.

I only barely noticed that we'd arrived at our floor... and that an older, immaculately dressed couple was gazing impatiently at us, just on the other side of the elevator doorway.

"A thousand pardons," I murmured to them, taking my woman by the arm and leading her between them.

Riley and I chuckled as we pulled ourselves down the hall and towards our room, paying the faintest attention to the suite numbers. As I tugged my card out and slid it into the doorknob reader, Riley's lips were more or less glued to my neck...

Until we stepped into the room, that was.

"...Holy shit," she blurted out.

The suite was a blend of contemporary sophistication and historical elegance, featuring dark wood tones with contrasting mocha and cream carpeting.

Along the wall above the magnificently deConnort king-sized bed, a backlit aquarium recessed into the wall, filled with beautiful tropical fish of extraordinary colours and breeds.

The thick, luscious drapes on the opposing wall were pulled aside and roped to the edges, revealing a large and jaw-dropping view of the very same nightlife we'd witnessed from the glass elevator.

Turning the corner, a luxury kitchen stood at attention, filled with various superfluous touches and leading down a couple of steps to a small spa area. Inside, I observed a steam room, a sauna, and a private Jacuzzi tub.

The bathroom was on the opposite side of the kitchen, up several steps and featuring an oversized glass shower room – with overhead recessed faucets to simulate perfect rainfall – and a lavish mirror above a marble sink countertop with Italian-style bowl sink.

"Good lord, Lex," Riley murmured to herself, taking in the sights as she quietly explored the suite. "This is fucking incredible… and exactly what I needed after the day I've had…"

"It *did* sound like something was the matter earlier, over our texts," I commented. "Do you want to tell me what happened?"

"I met Gloria Van Lark," she answered calmly. "She appeared in town and was seen in a few museums that featured my art... I had a confusing conversation with her."

"Oh? That's fantastic!" I grinned, before realizing the implications. "Wait... it doesn't sound like that went particularly well."

"She turned me down," Riley sadly told me. "I had my chance, and I blew it. She's gone."

"I'm sorry," I murmured, pulling her into an embrace and stroking her hair. "I know how much it meant to you to earn her respect... I'm sure you'll get another chance sometime. You've got a long career ahead of you, and you'll be in one of those galleries before you know it."

"It's funny, one of the visitors said something kind of like that..."

"Oh yeah?"

"Yeah. Someone who overheard and took pity on me after she saw the kind of effect meeting Gloria had on me… but anyway, that was earlier, and this is now. And *now* is… wonderful," she told me.

Riley glanced warmly up into my eyes and kissed me on the lips again. After a few seconds, she pulled out of my arms to admire the etched crown molding along the edges of the room.

"Did you seriously get this incredible suite for us tonight? It's absolutely amazing in here…"

"I wanted you to have a taste of deConnorce," I commented casually, stripping off my blazer and setting it on a hanger in the large walk-in closet. "Renting that small motel room down the other block is a modesty… *this* is something a little closer to my tastes."

"You're richer than I thought you were," she realized aloud, turning to me.

"*Richer* is relative. But does this change anything for you? Maybe how you feel about me?"

"Not a goddamn bit," she smiled, pulling me into a tight hug as she leaned up on her toes, planting her lips on mine…

Ten minutes later, the shower was running, her palms were against the glass wall, and mine were on her hips – as I bucked into them, again and again.

My lips found her throat and I groaned my satisfaction into the tender flesh, grazing my teeth along the edge.

She cooed in response, and I bit down, feeling her body murmur against me in complete, unadulterated delight. "Oh god, Lex," she whispered as the water drizzled down and the steam rose up around us. "You know how to fuck me so well…"

I released one hand to clutch a fistful of her hair, and I tugged backwards, holding her face up near the glass. Before the steam could completely cloud our vision, I forced her to watch us fucking in the large mirror, just a couple of yards straight ahead.

"That's right, just like that," she half-whispered, half-moaned. "Fuck me with your huge cock…"

At first, I ignored the request, relinquishing my grip on her skin and withdrawing from inside her. But before she could mutter her dislike, I changed my mind… and pulled her from the shower, wiping my feet off on the mat just outside.

Confident in the grip of my soles against the tile, I spun her around, lifting her up beneath her buttocks and supporting her against the glass wall. The water continued to drizzle on the other side of the glass as her ankles wrapped around my hips, clasped together into the small of my back.

"Oh wow… oh *fuck*," she groaned, enjoying the position as she realized what I had done. Now, she could rest against the wall, completely supported by my strength, and watch me plow into her again and again in the mirror.

"Lex… god*dammit*, Lex…"

My lips forced themselves down on hers, and I lifted her just a few degrees higher, giving myself a better angle to penetrate her on my cock. I loved how she was growing accustomed to the length, and within a few minutes of this, she was relaxed enough to allow my full length inside.

Once I was hilting her, feeling her slick, warm pussy clamp around my thick, throbbing tool, I felt my mind melt into a blissful paradise.

There were no stresses now.

No bellyaching publicist friend.

No rivals, dangling for what was mine.

No concerns over corporate contracts.

There was only the way that our bodies intermingled, our blood pumping through our veins as we fucked each other, so blissfully full of *life* and *passion*.

The sex I'd had before?

Mechanical. Just a means to an end, a way to release my own personal drug – a blinding mixture of endorphins and chemicals that flooded my head, giving me the high that let me forget all about the darkness in my past.

When I fucked, it all went away.

I could sleep at night... fitfully, sometimes, but at least it was something.

With Riley, though... it was as if an entirely new height was being reached. Even form the start, I'd felt something different about the ways our skin pressed together, and our bodies bent for one another.

I felt my restraints falling apart.

Riley was moaning at the top of her lungs now. I could feel her body tense up as she released a mighty scream, unimpeded by thin walls or the need for privacy. She let loose every ounce of strength she had, lost in the throes of passion as she came *hard* around my cock.

And as her pussy clenched, desperate to milk me dry, I felt my body grow rigid. I couldn't hold on any longer, and my limbs stiffened, pinning her into my embrace against the walls. Her fingertips were digging deep into my shoulders as my balls seized up, and I exploded with a roar of blinding ecstasy as my cock drained itself completely dry inside her – pumping the hardest, thickest, most voluminous orgasm I'd ever experienced in my entire life deep into her wet, sopping chasm.

She was experiencing a multiple orgasm around mine, and when her rapid heartbeat finally began to slow down, and her tense grip on my muscles started to relax, she looked me in the eyes with a completely defenseless gaze.

"Did… did we just come together?"

My chest was heaving as I nodded. "Yeah," I breathlessly responded. "I think so."

"Oh god, Lex, I didn't really think that could actually happen," she murmured in my ear, resting her chin onto my shoulder. "I mean, I've *heard* about that kind of thing, but it seemed so... unlikely... you know?"

I nodded again. "I know what you mean..."

Gently, I set her back to the ground, and we popped back into the shower to clean off the sweat from our furious fucking. We enjoyed the steam of the shower, taking our time in washing each other off, tracing the outlines of each other's bodies as we bathed one another.

Inevitably, one thing led to another, and I was taking her nipple between my teeth as her fingers wrapped lightly around my stiffening cock...

About two hours later, we were finally resting in bed, where we had finally wrapped up our marathon sex for the moment. My thoughts were ricocheting around in my head, and I felt the undying compulsion to finally speak my mind...

And to take a very dangerous step forward.

"What is it that you want, Riley?" I asked her as she ran her fingertips along my chest. "What do you want out of this?"

She turned her head, gazing fiercely into my eyes. I could sense such strength and determination in those retinas that they almost burned into my own.

"What do you mean?"

I paused, collecting my thoughts.

"We both know that I'm going back in a few weeks. I understand that your life is here… your friends are here… but… have you given any thought to…"

"To coming back with you?" Riley finished my question, her catlike gaze still focused intently on my eyes.

"Yes," I replied truthfully.

Riley maintained that gaze for a few moments, not speaking a single word. As the silence dragged out, she turned her head back, settling it against my chest again.

"So that's a no," I answered.

"That's a... deceitfully complicated question," Riley replied. "Everything that I know and love is here. Are you actually asking me to give it all up to return with you to England? My friendships, my life, and my entire world... it's here in New Orleans. You would ask me to drop it all?"

I realized the mistake I had made now.

I'd pushed her too hard.

I'd reached for too much.

"Ever since I was a little girl, I've wanted to go to England," Riley told me. "I grew up watching British sitcoms, classic episodes of *Doctor Who*. I can tell you all about Daleks and Cybermen and Ice Warriors... I can recount tales of Gallifrey and Skarro, of Davros and the Time Lords..."

"You know your stuff," I observed.

"You present an interesting opportunity," Riley thought aloud. "And I understand that this is a painless way to make a clean break. I can return with you and submerge myself in Great Britain, although that might set me back a little on the painting front..."

"You will have all the room you need to paint," I whispered.

"Is that so?"

"You should see Lambert House," I told her, recalling the estate fondly. "It stands proud and tall in the English countryside, down a long, winding road lined with beautiful trees…three stories tall with a sprawling basement and a massive attic, a thick wall all around for privacy, and magnificent gardens lining the front and the back… my cluster of orange trees bloom so brightly in the spring, growing the most delicious citrus you've ever tasted…"

"You paint a compelling argument," Riley whispered. "Will I have a studio?"

"I know just the room already," I thought wistfully. "On the west side of the house, with a great glass ceiling, where the sunlight catches just right no matter if you work at noon or sunset. The oranges and yellows of the horizon are so beautiful there, and you'll have enough space for a small gallery in that room alone… and a raised platform for your work."

"It sounds very beautiful," Riley murmured, closing her eyes to picture it. "Are there any closets?"

"Several," I answered, "clustered near the raised flooring. There's plenty of shelving, several bookcases... and ample light. You can store absolutely anything that you need, and if it's somehow not enough... I can always call out my contractors to install more space for you. Anything that you need."

"You actually mean that, don't you, Lex?"

"Absolutely."

Riley considered this carefully, her fingertips still stroking along my bare skin.

"Can my friends come to visit sometimes?"

"I see absolutely no reason why not."

She turned her face one last time, regarding me cautiously and carefully.

"Why me?" Riley finally asked.

I smiled. Answering that question something that didn't require even the slightest ounce of brainpower... because

I'd known the right response for a while now.

"Because you're not like the others Riley… Your art… Your mind… The way you make me feel when I see you… I'm always left wanting more."

"That's a nice little speech there," she chuckled. "Kind of convincing, too. Have you always been this silver-tongued?"

"I've had a lot of time to think about this."

Riley seemed to accept that reply.

"You realize, of course," she told me, "that in order for me to join you back abroad… I can't just be your partner, or your girlfriend, or your friend with benefits. I need my art, Lex, and I won't give up my business. Getting a work visa in the UK is nearly impossible. Even money can't cut through all the red tape. It might be years before I can get the necessary paperwork, and the damage that would do… I can't pursue my work there unless…"

"Unless you were my wife."

"It's not going to be that easy. I expect more from people who are asking me to make that plunge with them.

You're going to have to propose your *ass* off if you want any remote chance that I'll agree to something this crazy. I barely know you Lex."

"You could look me up, if you really wanted to," I said quietly. It was all there online... My checkered history... My indiscretions...

"I guess I was just enjoying the surprises... A part of me didn't want to know who you are," she replied quietly.

"If you won't look, let me tell you the most important thing."

A faint, deviant smile crossed her lips.

"I love you, Riley."

Chapter 11
Riley

A couple of blissful afternoons later came the day that things finally came crashing down with Lex. Unaware of the things to come, I wandered into Connor's record store with Reiko by my side, ready to answer a strange text message to drop by.

He was busy running some paperwork in the back, so Reiko and I perused some of the records. Even if he had a misguided jealousy complex, I couldn't ignore the fact that Connor had extremely great tastes when it came to music.

Probably why he drew so much of the local talent… and the bigger names that passed through town, playing their venues. More than one legendary secret show had happened within the basement beneath this record store.

When Connor finally popped out from the back, his eyes immediately zeroed in on me. He called his assistant over and waved his hands around animatedly, clearly telling her off under his breath.

I could imagine why, although it didn't please me that he was so hard on her. She was helping other customers, after all.

She looked absolutely downtrodden as she returned to help a pair of punks check out some vintage material. Meanwhile, Connor waved us both over, and we followed him towards the back of the store.

Passing through the beaded curtain along the doorway behind the counter, he guided us past a couple of storage rooms and to his main office. We leaned against the wall, avoiding the various tables that were buried under spare record sheaths and mountains of paperwork, while Connor slipped around the back of his small, beaten desk.

"What kind of favor did you need?" I asked him, crossing my arms.

"Actually, I just said that to get you to come over, although I was kind of hoping that we'd be... alone..." he glanced over at Reiko guiltily.

She sighed and rolled her eyes.

"Why's that, Will?" I demanded, just waiting on him to fuck this up. What he did next… I could never have seen coming.

"So, I looked into this Lex of yours," he started, pushing his glasses up the bridge of his nose.

"You don't have to say anything Connor. I already know he's wealthy…"

"Wealthy is part of it… He's a goddamned celebrity."

"A celebrity?" I asked, my curiosity piquing.

"Yeah… he's a huge deal in England, actually. He's not just *any* soccer player, he's basically *the* soccer player… captain of what they call the National team, sort of a football super-group that represents the entire country in the international World Cup Series."

"Oh shit, *seriously?*" Reiko chimed in. "That's wicked cool!" She elbowed me lightly in the ribs, a massive smile across her face. "What a fucking catch, girl!"

"I knew he played… But… The World Cup? Are you sure about this?" I asked, pensively.

"Yeah. He's been playing with them for a couple of years now. Before then, he was in some of the major teams, so he's what you might think of as a national icon. The audiences love him. He's one of the best players in the world... handsome, charming... and absolutely great with the fans."

"So, why do you care?" Reiko asked, tilting her head. "We all know that you've been pissed off about this guy for a few weeks... have you finally come around, or what?"

Connor's face darkened.

"No, actually, because there's more to it."

"What, is he a fucking *astronaut, too?*" Reiko chuckled. "Does he play that sport on the goddamn moon?"

"No," Connor gravely answered. "He stays relevant to pop culture for his skills, his charm... and his reputation."

"What *kind* of reputation?" I asked.

Before he could respond, I was already dreading the answer. My stomach began to turn as he quietly hid the fact that he was *relishing* this fucking moment… that meant that, whatever I was about to learn?

It was going to be bad.

Really bad.

"Instead of telling you, I should probably just *show* you," Connor replied carefully, reaching for a nearby manila folder. He scattered a couple of sheets off of it, retrieving it from a nearby pile of documents, and unsheathed a stapled stack of papers before handing them to me.

As I glanced down at what I was seeing, my blood began to completely boil.

Each page was a different printout of a British tabloid cover or interior article. On every page, there was a large snapshot of Lex Lambert in a compromising position, with a sensationalist headline that put his exploits front and center:

Lightning Lex Caught with Innocent Starlet!

Lambert Throws Destructive Hotel Orgy!

Lightning Strikes Again! Now with Two Co-eds!

Lightning Lambert's Beach Sex-capades!

Lex's New Record: One Night, Five Dancers!

I flipped through page after page of his sexual exploits, each one more ridiculous than the last. Paparazzi shots with tasteful blurring adorned the package of files that Connor had handed me, and I could barely make it two-thirds through before I just skimmed the rest and sank to the floor.

The two of them remained silent.

Reiko took the folder from my quaking hands and skimmed through the pages, and then sighed as she set it down beside my ankle.

"Well… I guess nobody's perfect," she mumbled. "I'm really sorry, Riley."

I clenched my fists, opening and closing them repeatedly. "I can't believe I trusted him so implicitly," I spat out between my grinding teeth. "How could I be such a goddamn idiot?"

"You're not an idiot, sweetie," Reiko tried to comfort me. She placed a hand on my shoulder and rubbed it lightly. "You just trust people. You take them at their word sometimes. And, to be fair, that guy is *hella* hot. It's no wonder you're just finding out about this now."

"Why?" I asked nobody in particular, scraping the heels to my shoes across the tile. "I knew his name. Why didn't I bother to even remotely check on him?"

"Google is a beautiful thing," Connor commented dryly. "I'm just glad I looked into this before it got any more serious."

I flashed him an ugly stare, and Reiko immediately took in a quick breath of air.

"Will," she mentioned, "now's not a good–"

"You didn't do this because you were looking out for me," I accused him, rising up the length of the wall and stepping towards him. "You did this because you're jealous of him. We all know you've got a huge crush on me. I get it. You're pissy that I found someone else. You've been passive-aggressive over Lex for weeks."

"Wait, Riley–" He tried to blurt out.

"No. Fuck it all. You *love* that he's got these fucking skeletons in his closet.

It takes him out of the running so that, what, you can swoop right in and rescue me when I need you? What kind of white knight bullshit were you thinking?"

"Riley," Reiko tried to intervene. "I think you're being a bit hard on him–"

"Stay out of this, Reiko," I commanded her before turning back to him. Connor simply stood there, seated on the edge of the desk and staring at me with sadness staining his eyes.

"Of course I'm fucking mad that this has happened. But I'm angrier still with *you*. *You* didn't bring this to my attention out of the kindness of your heart, and we all know it. You did this to get a leg up on him.

"Well, spoiler alert, Will. You're a good guy, but I'm not into you. I've *never* been into you. And I never will be. You're like a brother to me. You know this. How many times do I have to tell you?"

Connor swallowed, and rose up from his desk. He turned around and faced the large David Bowie poster up behind his desk – the single piece of decoration in his office.

"Please go," he half-croaked.

"Will…" Reiko whispered after him.

"I need to be alone," he insisted miserably. "When you go, please tell Tiana to lock up and excuse herself for the day. I'll give her a full shift's pay."

I grunted my approval of that response, reaching down to snatch up the folder of revelations into Lex's past. As I stood up, I noticed that neither of them had budged an inch.

"Are you coming, Reiko?"

She didn't turn away from him.

"Reiko?"

"No, I… go ahead without me," she spoke.

I suppressed a deep, angry sigh, and passed down the hallway and towards the front. Tiana had just finished ringing up the two punks, and they were traipsing back out of the store, leaving just us.

I relayed the message to her, and she avoided eye contact with me. It seemed that she'd probably heard some of the exclamations from the back, so I shook my head bitterly and let her lock me outside as she flipped the *Open* sign around.

By the time the streetcar got me to the end of my street, the sun was already beginning to set on the horizon. I called ahead to a Chinese takeout place further up the road, and stepped in to pay and take my dinner home with me.

I was expecting Lex for the evening, like usual. He had told me he would be running a little later than usual, as he was training harder today for his upcoming football season.

He always loved to fuck me on training days.

Tonight, was going to be a little different than what he expected.

It was an hour later that he walked through the door to my apartment. I'd just wrapped up dinner and cleaned up the place, and I was perched comfortably on the couch in front of the TV when he let himself in.

"Ello, Riley," he chuckled to himself as he stepped into the living room. His expression fell as he took in my glaring face, and his gaze shifted to the stack of pages on the corner of my coffee table.

From his angle, he undoubtedly recognized the top sheet… and that explained why he turned to me with a careful, fearful look.

"Riley, I think we should talk–"

I cut him off, leaping up from my seat.

"When were you planning on telling me that you're publicly known as a womanizing asshole?" I demanded to know, throwing the stapled stack of papers into his face. "Or that you've been caught fucking your way across the tabloids for years?"

With the reflexes of a trained athlete, Lex snatched the fluttering pack of papers from the air, flipping backwards and forwards between the pages.

"I can explain," Lex stiffly offered.

"I seriously doubt that."

"If you'll give me a moment–"

"You know, I knew there was more to you, but I never expected this," I bitterly told him. "And here it is. How many sex scandals have you been a part of?"

"You tell me," he said sharply. "You appear to have done your research. What I'm wondering is why you've dug this all up *now*, of all times…"

"I *didn't*," I defiantly exclaimed.

"Then how…?"

"My friends. They look out for me. They pulled you up online and dug up all this crap on you. What the *hell*, Lex? What else have you been hiding from me?"

"I enjoy my privacy, and last I remember you didn't care about my past," he wearily answered.

"Certain things you reveal to the strangers you whisk up into your arms," I angrily rebutted. "Such as the fact that you've fucked your way across half of the United Kingdom. Or that you're apparently a World Cup player?"

He paused with a groan.

"Do you even know what that means?"

"Of course I do, Lex. I *did my research*, remember? I looked up how big a deal that was. You led me to believe that you were just some football player on some rinky-dink team in England."

Lex's eyes instantly flared into rage.

"Excuse me, what the fuck did you just say?"

If I wasn't so bitterly angry, and with the moral high ground solidly beneath my feet, I might have been intimidated. His eyes were wild with fury, and he took a menacing step towards me, and another, until he was so close that I could practically feel the heat pumping off of his body.

"Don't you dare – *dare* – insult my sport, my place in it, or the teams that I've had the privilege of representing."

"Oh, *boo the fuck hoo*," I mocked him. "You think you're such hot shit? Well, maybe you are. Maybe I would have taken you a bit more seriously if you'd been honest with me, instead of pretending to blend in as some minor football player with some money in the bank having a little fun on vacation."

"I'm a big fucking deal back home, alright? Is that what you want to hear? I can't take a shit without some arse paparazzi taking a picture through my window. I'm angling for a contract that will put my face on every piece of merchandising beneath the Patrovo Corporation."

"The Patro – *what now*?"

"The corporation that owns a third of the country," Lex snarled. "I'm here to get away from that life – to keep myself out of trouble. I'll be considered as their corporate mascot for the year. It's a twenty-million pound sponsorship... and I'm facing a rival who can rip it all away from beneath me."

"Aren't you already rich?" I snapped. "Why is it that the greedy just keep getting greedier?"

"I'm beloved by the English populace," Lex responded, glaring down at me. "I'm a cultural icon. But it's not just that... I'm one of the best fucking players in the world. I've been world-class material for *years*. And now I *deserve* this. It's not about the money. Do you think Michael Jordan cares about the money? This is about immortality. *This sponsorship is my reward.*"

"Your reward for *what*, exactly? Kicking a ball around better than the other guys? Keeping your pants down so often that you're in dozens of tabloid issues? Making a complete fucking fool of yourself?"

Lex advanced, and I pressed my back up against the wall. I bitterly returned his furious glare, letting a sly smile cross my lips.

"You could have had everything Riley. I'd have given you *everything*. I thought you were different."

"I am different! Do you think that's what I'm after? Your money?"

"That's not what I meant," Lex began, but I cut him off.

"I didn't even know who you were until today. You're *not* the only badass in the room. Dozens of galleries carry my art. I drew the attention of one of the most legendary museum curators in the world. I'm an accomplished, award-winning, decorated painter about to hit world-class… in my *mid-twenties*. I've got *decades* ahead of me to hone and sharpen my craft and all it takes is for *one* painting to take off at auction, and everything I've ever touched will be priceless."

Lex stood there, silent.

"How long can you kick a fucking ball around on the field, Lex? How long will *your* career last? I checked the statistics. The usual professional athlete career lasts eight, maybe ten years even at the highest level. You've already been on the field professionally for years now. What are you going to do when the sun sets on your glory days, huh?"

Lex lowered his face down to mine, and I realized in that second just how far I'd pushed him... I didn't know if he was going to kiss me or hit me, and I wasn't sure which of those two things I was more afraid of... If he put his lips on mine, would I be able to stop him? Would I want to?

"Fuck you, Riley," he growled in a deep, dark voice, baritones lower than I'd ever heard from him. "You've crossed the line."

He pulled back to look at me quietly. One palm came down from the wall, and then the other. He stood there, regarding me quietly for a moment, and finally took a step backwards.

I summoned up every ounce of strength I kept down in my core. "I really need you to leave."

Lex looked pained, as if I'd just stabbed him straight in the heart. He took another stumbling step backwards, glancing down at his open palms, and searched my eyes with a glance.

"*Now*, Lex."

"No," he murmured. "We can fix this. I know you have feelings for me."

"Lex."

I let my face darken as I took a step towards him. "You've betrayed my trust. I just want you *out* of my apartment and *out* of my life."

"Please, Riley," he whispered.

I'd had enough of his bullshit.

"You haven't listened to a fucking word I've said, have you, Alexander Lambert?" I jeered. "You're *trespassing* now. Get out."

He realized then that I wasn't backing down, and his eyes narrowed at me. He didn't even bother to cast out one last, pathetic *please.*

All I knew was that I wanted him gone. He could come back later, maybe, after I'd cooled down and had some time to take in all of this new information – about his past, about his reputation, about everything.

But for right now? He had to go. I needed some space and some time.

With one last, withered look – a look that boiled into relentless anger – Lex Lambert slammed the front door behind him, disappearing into the night.

Chapter 12
Lex

When I stormed out of her apartment, I wasn't thinking straight. All that I knew was that I needed to get out of that place and away from her.

The painful, vicious things she'd said.

The buried memories she'd drudged up.

I needed to blow some steam, and fast.

While wandering along the French Quarter, surrounded by bar upon bar, I gave some serious consideration to popping into any one of them and drinking myself into a blinding stupor.

Luckily, I was thinking clearly enough to recognize how fucking awful an idea that would be. I could imagine Jess's furious face, screaming obscenities at me:

What if you're caught on camera?

What if they drag you out to the street?

What if you hurt *somebody?*

Grow the fuck up, Lex!

With a low growl and an absent-minded wave of my wrist, I banished the apparition from my thoughts. Sure, Jess was going to be pissed – both as my best friend *and* my publicist – but I couldn't help but require some time to simmer down.

That was, even if I *did* keep her fears in mind. After all, if she knew where I was and what I was doing at the time… I was aware that her perceived thoughts on the matter weren't exactly incorrect.

My eyes scanned the windows of another bar as I passed by. This one, however, caught my eye. Two words: *billiards tables.*

I allowed myself a sliver of a smile.

Now… there's *a thought.*

My heel turned, and I found myself strolling into the bar. The bouncer at the front, some fat fuck picking his teeth, let his jaw slacken as he spotted me.

"Whoa, partner," he shook his head. "Not sure this is exactly your kind of place… whatcha want from in here?"

"Pool table," I grunted.

"Lots of places in town with a pool table," he observed, lifting his chin to stare me down his fat, pudgy nose. "Places more suited to a man of yer, uh, refined tastes…"

"Where's the closest one?"

"Dunno."

"Well, then," I smiled, "that's just too far."

He shook his head lightly. "Suit yerself."

I gave him a slight nod of acknowledgement as I passed into the bar. I could see why he had tried to steer me elsewhere. This was a bit of a rougher place: darker, grittier, and with an obvious change in clientele. Black leather and cut, plaid jackets dominated the scene… a scene in which I stood out like a sore thumb.

But I was already committed to the course.

A few pairs of eyes wound up on me as I passed through the entrance, and those eyes belonged to men who elbowed those to their side. Within moments, like a great wave of attention, half the bar was staring at me.

None of them seemed to be making trouble. No one stepped into my way or brushed against my shoulder; nobody called me out or shouted for me.

See? I thought to myself. *These gentlemen know how to be civilized.*

I stepped towards the bar, pushing a bar stool aside and falling into place near a great, slovenly man and his equally fat wife. Dressed in comically undersized cowboy/girl attire, they studied me carefully and gnawed on what was either gum or, more likely, chewing tobacco.

"Bourbon, neat," I requested.

"Well?" The bartender tried to clarify.

"Yeah. Sure."

A bigger, grizzlier guy himself, the bartender nodded once. He dropped a few cubes into a tumbler and poured some whiskey over it, and I handed him some cash.

"Yer change, sir."

"Eh," I closed an eye at him, quickly gritting my teeth in thought. "Keep it."

He looked dumbfounded for a moment. I might have accidentally handed him a twenty instead of a ten, not that it was particularly any skin off of my back. After all, I was still getting used to American currency, even with the big numbers in the corners.

I downed the drink and requested another, being certain to tip him a little more appropriately. This one, I carried over to the only free pool table around.

Digging around in the pockets, I withdrew the lost pool balls and racked them all up. Buffing the tip of a cuestick with the chalk, I dusted my hands, then broke the pyramid and began to play myself.

My residual frustration with the events of the night was throwing me off my game, but I managed to keep the cue ball from flying off the table. Still, my playing was substantially less than ideal, and I was starting to think that I was embarrassing myself.

I lost a game or two with other players before I really started to finally hit my stride. Guiding my anger into careful precision strikes, I began dominating the corner. My resolve strengthening with each turn, I continued proving to myself that I was the reigning alpha on more green fields than one.

An hour passed as I downed another two, maybe three drinks. My playing continued improving, surprisingly enough. I was starting to draw some attention from the other tables, and players began watching me instead of their opponents during their games.

I was keeping an eye on some of them, too, and this particular kid caught my focus. He was a really sloppy player, scattering the balls poorly and accidentally ricocheting the cue ball off the table on more than one occasion. Some of us started to chuckle at his ineptitude, although I noticed the passion in his eyes for the sport.

Give it a few years, kid, I thought to myself. *With dedication like yours, you'll get good at this...*

The cue ball sailed off the table again.

...Eventually.

It was after that game finished that I noticed him handing bills to the other player, a look of dejection and defeat across his face. *He's gambling? Is he hoping Lady Luck will kiss his cheek?*

My opponent bought me a drink after I won, and the kid crossed my path. By now, he'd played just about everyone near the pool tables, and I was the single contender left.

"Want a round?" He asked.

I studied him for a moment.

"Nah, kid. I'm good."

"You sure?" He asked. "I'll bet ya a hundred bucks."

"Hundred dollars, eh?" I asked, sizing him up with different eyes. "That's more than you've been giving the others…"

"Dad's rich. I just enjoy playing with his money, even if I'm not too great at this," he shrugged. "I think I'm starting to get a hang for it."

"You want some pointers?" I asked.

"Much obliged… but I'm one of those 'learn as I go' types," he smiled toothily and scratched the back of his head. "I've gotta let my body figure it all out by itself, and then I just do whatever winds up working."

"Muscle memory," I acknowledged, nodding to myself. "I know what you're talking about. Friends of mine are the same way."

"So, you want a round, or nah?"

I scoffed. "...Fine. One round."

"Sweeten the pot?"

"Don't need to," I shook my head.

"Oh, come on, bro," he chided me. "Guy in a nice suit like you? You can afford to piss away a hundred bucks, losing to me."

Something clicked in my head. Looking back on it, it was less like an idea popping, and more like disarming the safety on a revolver.

"That's a lot of smack, coming from a kid with your losing streak," I grinned. A few other patrons nearby were taking interest, nodding their approval.

"Put yer money where yer mouth is."

I dug into my front pocket and whipped out my wallet, glancing through and pushing the wad of hundreds aside, looking for some twenties. I counted out a hundred in the sheath and slipped it back into place.

"Alright, kid. Hundred bucks," I agreed. "What about you? You've been bleeding dollars all night. What have you got left?"

He slipped his hand into his pocket and showed me a handful of crumpled twenties. "I'm good for it," the kid nodded.

"What's your name?" I asked, setting us up for a fresh game. "I like to know my opponents when I face them on the green."

"On the green?" He asked, shaking his head. "That's a weird way with words you've got yerself there... name's Dylan. You?"

I thought for a moment. "Alex."

"Alex," he nodded. "Well, Alex, ready to get your butt whooped?"

An amused smile crossed my lips. "By all means, friend." I lifted the triangle, leaving a perfectly shaped pyramid of balls in position, and set the cue ball right into place. I stepped back, waving towards the table with my wrist.

"Ladies first," I goaded.

Dylan's face fell. "Ain't no lady."

"Prove it."

A sly smile spread across his face, and he buffed the end of his cue stick. Spectating players stepped aside as he strolled over into position, lined up his shot, and broke the triangle... knocking two solids straight into their pockets, and leaving complete disarray that put stripes at a disadvantage.

My teeth gritted as I surveyed the aftermath with a second's glance. *That's not luck that made that shot work...*

I tried to line something useful up, but it wasn't happening. Instead, I decided to knock some of the balls further around, and spent my turn splintering the battleground.

Dylan took advantage of this, knocking another solid into the pocket. His shot sent a second one towards the corner, but it hovered near the edge of the hole – clearly lined up for another perfect shot.

"You've hustled me," I acknowledged. I couldn't really be angry. I'd fallen hard for his little ploy. Some of the patrons chuckled in agreement; after all, they'd already made some money off of the kid, and it was all at the expense of the suited, foreign newcomer.

Dylan looked wounded. "Just a few lucky ones, man. I knew my fortunes would change, sooner or later…"

I didn't buy it for a second, even as I sank in a striped ball per turn. With each successive move, Dylan blocked me, sent one or two balls in, or completely fucked my approach. When he got to the eight ball, he banked it off three bumpers before burying it in the corner pocket, just to be an ass.

And he was smiling wide as can be.

"You got me Dylan," I said, tossing the twenties on the table. "Well played."

Dylan didn't move. He looked down at the money like I'd just insulted him.

"What the fuck is that?"

I looked back at the table, the five twenties spread across the green felt.

"That's one hundred dollars. Don't spend it all in one place, kid."

He took a step toward me, then another. I stared down at the scrawny kid as he grabbed my shirt, twisting it in his fist. "We were playing for the thousand dollars you've got in that fucking wallet of yours."

I almost wanted to laugh in his face. I could crush this kid. I could kick him hard enough to send him sailing across this godforsaken bar. I reached up and peeled his hand free, holding his wrist in the air.

"So you're a hustler and a thief?" I asked, anger starting to well up inside me. The little prick thought he could jack up the bet now that the game was over?

The other players – most of who weren't even playing anymore – shifted uncomfortably or hesitantly moved closer. In response, I released his hand, holding my hands up in restraint.

"Take your money, and get away from me."

"Pay me what we agreed on," the kid shouted.

"Your money is on the table. Sod off." I replied, turning away. I was finished with this discussion. I wanted to get back to my drink and forget any of this happened.

I had no such luck.

A hand gripped my shoulder and spun me round. Before I could react, the kid's pitiful little fist made contact with my chin. I stared at him in disbelief. I'd grown up on the streets. I'd been in my fair share of fights in and out of the bars and I'd never seen someone throw such a weak arse punch.

"You little piece of shit!" I shouted, thrusting a quick jab into his face. I didn't want to hurt the kid, I just wanted to bloody his nose a bit and teach him a damn lesson. What happened next was something right off the green. Dylan fell backwards and exaggeratedly flung himself across a pool table as if I'd just hit him with a goddamned truck. He was screaming and flopping on the floor. The kid was faking it!

What the hell?

Another set of arms wrapped themselves around me. I wrenched an arm free and left a glancing blow against the redneck. Two more people tackled me to the ground. I went into self defense mode, arms and legs flailing until a flash of a badge came across my vision and I realized that an officer of the law was attempting to restraining me against the ground.

"You're coming with me," he snarled into my ear. Every drop of adrenaline pulsing through my veins left when I felt the cold, constraining sensation of handcuffs around my wrists.

"Wait – no!" I started to growl.

"You have the right to remain silent," the officer began, pulling me up to a stand. "Anything you say can and will be used against you in a court of law…"

I looked up, catching the kid's eyes. He was grinning wide as he strode toward the door at the back of the bar. It was only then that I noticed my wallet in his hand. The little arse had pickpocketed me, and used the "fight" to cover his tracks!

"Wait! That little shit!"

The officer pulled my arms up tighter behind me, forcing a shout of pain and cutting me off. He continued rattling off my rights as I was pulled towards the front exit. The patrons were giving me a wide berth, regarding me impartially, but a face in the crowd caused my heart to stop on the spot.

No… it can't be.

The unmistakable grin of Alistair Pritch filled my vision, draining the life from my limbs. I staggered, almost dropping to my knees, as the officer helped keep me upright.

You see, I had realized in that very instant what had happened to me tonight.

"You…" I gasped in defeat.

My enemy simply nodded, standing directly in front of me, his wicked smile spreading wider across his lips.

"That's right, Lex. I've been waiting a long time to see you in handcuffs… and now, I finally had my opportunity. You're an easy man to follow, did you know that?"

"Stand back, sir," the officer told him as he tugged me along.

"Enjoy seeing me on a cereal box soon, Lex!" Alistair chuckled menacingly, blending back into the crowd. "And enjoy your night in jail!"

He did this, I thought to myself. *He set me up. He must have paid the kid to play me like a goddamn fool… but why is he here? And how did he find me?*

I knew, as the officer dragged me outside and towards his squad car, that I'd have plenty of time to consider these questions.

I also knew that the answers wouldn't come.

Chapter 13

Riley

When I climbed into the passenger seat of Jess's rental sedan, I was still seething with anger from the earlier argument with Lex.

Him getting arrested hadn't helped matters.

…Even if I felt personally a little responsible.

Jess didn't say anything at first, as we navigated through the streets and headed towards the parish prison. Instead, we sat in silence, quietly watching the rain sprinkle absentmindedly against the windshield.

"I think this is the first chance we've had to really speak together," Jess finally spoke up, keeping her eyes locked onto the road.

"That implies that we've been speaking," I observed, glancing over at her.

A small grin crossed her face.

"He really fucked up this time, didn't he?" Jess asked.

"Well, he's in jail…"

"That's not what I mean," Jess replied. "With you, I mean. I haven't seen him so easygoing in years… For him to storm off into the night like this? To get into a fight? Lex has been the center of plenty of scandals, but he hasn't been in a straight up bar fight since his early career… You two must have been in one hell of an argument."

"That's not really your business," I shrugged.

Even in the darkness, I sensed Jess's face harden into bitter resolve. "It actually *is* my business," she quickly replied. "It's my job."

"Your job? You represent him, right? You're his agent or whatever? So what if we had a little spat?" I told her, challenging her darkened tone with my own. *Who the fuck does she think she is, anyway?* "Whatever goes on between us is none of your concern, like I said."

The car screeched to a halt.

"I'm not his agent, Riley. I don't land him gigs or whatever the fuck you think an agent for an athlete does. I'm his fucking publicist."

"Publicist?" I asked, creasing my brow. "You've been doing an *excellent* job with that, then. Because a friend of mine spent thirty minutes in Google and pulled up a treasure trove of disaster on your client."

"Lex Lambert is a World Cup football player," she told me, staring at me with wide, wild eyes. "He's one of the best players on the fucking planet of the most popular sport in the entire world. He's also a loose cannon and a complete fucking prick, and he makes my life a tremendous hell."

"Then, why do you bother representing him? Is it just because he's loaded?"

"*Because* Alexander Lambert saved my life, you nosy little shit," Jess angrily told me.

"What?" I asked, feeling a sudden burst of shame that I'd turned on him… after he'd rescued *me* in my time of need.

Jess's eyes glistened with tears.

"We met while we were both homeless. We relied on each other to survive. When he started pulling himself up and making a name for in the junior leagues, he didn't for get about me. He immediately pulled me off the streets.

"While he slept on a tiny fucking cot in the den, he insisted that I have a bedroom – with a locking door. He protected me. He never laid a finger on me or asked for anything. He was my best friend... Maybe my only friend. With his help, I followed in his footsteps. I got myself into a good university, and found a career that I love... one that allows me to return the fucking favor."

We sat in silence for a moment, allowing us to hear the chorus of honks from behind. Muttering something under her breath, Jess finally kicked the car back into drive, and we tore down the roads on our way to where he was imprisoned.

"I had no idea," I muttered.

"Of course you didn't," she snapped. "He's a good fucking man, even if he's a complete, unrepentant pain in the ass ... If he could just learn to get a grip of himself, he'd have that stupid fucking sponsorship in the bag..."

"I had to find out myself that he's such a big deal," I responded. "He lied to me and practically told me that he was a nobody. Why the fuck didn't he *say* anything?"

"Because he was *supposed* to be laying low," Jess answered through gritted teeth. "And now he's been arrested in a foreign country for instigating a barroom brawl." She sighed, running her fingers through her hair. "Goddammit… I can't make this one go away."

"Yeah, *why* was he arrested?" I thought to ask. "You didn't say much over the phone earlier…"

Jess glanced at me for a second, before turning back to the road and answering. "When he left your apartment, he found himself a bar with some pool tables. The cops say he attacked somebody."

"That doesn't sound like Lex," I said.

"No… It doesn't," Jess replied. "He's been in a few fights, but never one *he* started. He's a lover, not a fighter."

I shook my head, the tabloid covers flashing through my mind. A *lover* indeed…

"And *you're* the one who fucked up," Jess added.

"*I* fucked up?" I spat out, turning to glare at her with every ounce of enmity I could muster. *Seriously though – who the* fuck *does she think she is?*

"Yes, *you* fucked up," she reiterated. "What, so, you're upset that he was hiding some things from you, right? Is that it?"

"That's all the reason I need… and for the record, I *still* don't see how it's any of your goddamn business, publicist or not," I answered.

It was Jess's turn to be furious.

"Alright, *smartass,* did it ever occur to you to question what an obviously rich, well-dressed Englishman was *doing* without a day job in America?" She asked, glancing over at me.

Before I could respond, she continued:

"He wears tailored handmade Italian suits, plays a little *soccer* as you'd call it, and he's just flying under the radar. Here I was, thinking he was completely fucking obvious. I mean… you knew his name. You didn't bother to look him up? You could have had any of these answers at any point. Hell, did you ever *directly* ask him who he was and what he did?"

"Why would I have done that? I don't have any reason to snoop around on the guy," I answered. "Not until someone else did it for me, not that I *asked* for the help or anything…"

"So, what, you're the one woman in the world who wouldn't be suspicious about any of those details? The man is a sex god, do you think he wouldn't have a little history? No… You know what I think? I think you were never looking for a real relationship. You were using Lex. You wanted a little fun for the night and you didn't *care* who he was. I've seen the way he looks at you. That man loves you! How do you feel? Did you ever tell him how you really felt? Did you let him know he was nothing but a shag?"

We took a sharp turn, and I braced myself against the armrest on the door.

"Maybe that *was* what I wanted… But things changed," I replied, my anger turning to sadness.

"You know, Lex can be a *real* fucking prick," Jess said, "but he's a good guy underneath. You brought that out in him. You were *good* for him. I don't think I've ever seen him happier.

And don't sit there and pretend you don't want things to work out. You wouldn't be coming if you didn't want to see him."

"I'm just here for the moral support, and then I'm right the fuck out of here."

"Seriously?" She tilted her head and glanced over at me.

"I don't need his money, or his lifestyle."

We came to a stop, and I realized that we were finally here. Jess killed the engine and turned to me again, her uninterrupted gaze piercing through mine.

"Let's get one thing straight, you and I. I happen to think that you're a smart woman with a great head on your shoulders. I know you're not after his damn money! Do you think I'd have let him go near you if you were some kind of piece of shit gold digger?"

I went silent as the car came to a stop. While I deliberated on these thoughts, I followed Jess into the station. She opened the door for me, and we walked up to the front desk clerk. With bushy gray hair and a stern face, the clerk seemed faintly familiar, but I couldn't place him.

"I'm here for Alexander Lambert," Jess confidently informed him. "He should be incarcerated here somewhere for drunken disorderly conduct of some sort."

The clerk glanced up from his desk.

"British guy, right?"

"That's the one!" She chirpily smiled

"Right. He won't be able to leave just yet," the clerk responded, glancing through a file on his desk. "We're waiting to see if the young man he assaulted wishes to press charges."

"I'm sure that an amicable solution can be found," Jess responded instantly, her smile unwaveringly strong.

"Be that as it may… we still need to keep him here while we finish receiving eyewitness accounts. There's an officer taking down notes as we speak."

"May I speak to this kid? I'm sure I can make an arrangement with him to handle this without tying up your valuable time…"

"Afraid not," the clerk told us. "We haven't found him yet. We're interviewing witnesses as we speak."

"…Virgil?" I asked, letting it all come back to me. "Virgil Higgins, is that you?"

The clerk blinked a few times, and then recognized me. "Riley Ricketts… didn't expect to see you here. What brings you in here?"

"My boyfriend appears to be in your jail," I shrugged. "This is his friend, Jess. We're trying to figure out what to do about this *alleged* act of his. Is there anything we can do?"

"Nothing outside of wait for a phone call," the clerk noted hesitantly.

As if on cue, the phone on Virgil's desk rang, and he paused to answer.

We caught part of a one-sided conversation, although he cupped the receiver in his palm at one point and turned away. Both of us leaned closer to hear, although it was of no use.

He hung up and turned back to us.

"Looks like it's your lucky day… Detective Donovan has three witnesses that say the other guy threw the first punch, and one of them just backed up Lex's story that the kid made off with his wallet. We're gonna go ahead and drop the charges. Your boyfriend is free to go," Virgil told us. "Now, normally he'd wind up at the back of the list, and get out late morning… but for you, darling, I can expedite him out shortly."

"Much obliged, Virgil," I smiled.

"Not a problem. My wife loves the paintings you've put in our living room. She swears by your work."

"Happy to contribute. Tell Mary-Ann that I send all of my love."

"Will do, darling."

We waited outside in the sedan for a few minutes. Finally, an officer escorted Lex out of the building and removed his handcuffs, pointing towards our vehicle.

When he climbed into the car, he gave me a quick glance of acknowledgment. I wasn't sure how much of my irritation to convey, so I simply kept a strong, impartial face.

Jess, meanwhile, immediately slapped him.

"Do you have *any idea* how difficult you just made my job for me, with that bullshit stunt of yours?"

"A… little?" Lex asked, nursing his cheek.

"Arrested! *Arrested, on battery charges and disorderly conduct!* What the fuck, Lex? How the shit do I spin that to Brett Barker?"

"Maybe he doesn't have to know. They dropped the charges Jess."

"They're going to know. They're probably printing up tomorrows tabloid as we speak. 'Lex arrested for beating American youth!', what the hell were you thinking?"

"There's something you don't know," he elaborated, his eyes still focused on her. "I was setup. Alistair Pritch was in the crowd, and he knew *exactly* what was happening."

"Alistair Pritch… is *here?*" Jess asked.

"The one and only," he continued. "He was there in the crowd, grinning like a goddamn fool. He paid that kid to start a fight with me and take a fall. He played me like a damn fiddle."

"You're certain," Jess asked.

"Yeah. Why?"

"Because Alistair should be in England right now… I'm going to have to check in on that and see what I can pull up…"

"Who the fuck is Alistair Pritch?" I finally asked. Whoever he was… if he was here in town, and they were *that* bothered by this fact, then I figured I should have a little knowledge about him.

"Alistair is one of my teammates," Lex answered. "He's an old rival from back when we were on opposing teams. Right now, he's a subordinate on the National team, but he's clearly angling for my sponsorship contract… and he's followed me here to set me up."

"Why would somebody do that?" I asked.

"Wouldn't be the first time," Jess said. "Last time the tabloids had a spread on Lex only two people knew where he was holed up, me and Alistair. It was no coincidence the paparazzi showed up."

"He wants my sponsorship… And he's going to get it."

They spent the car ride back discussing a plan of action for containing the aftermath of the arrest.

Worries for another day, he'd said, although Jess seemed rather less than convinced.

Jess dropped us off at the curb by my apartment. "It's only a brief walk if you need to come back," she told him before giving me a wink. "Try to keep him from getting into any more trouble tonight, yeah?"

"I'll do my best," I responded.

She headed off into the night, and the two of us stood in silence at the door to my apartment building. Lex scraped the toe of his sole against the pavement, wrists in his pockets. He looked so different now. Was I really going to do this? Could I really just let all of this go and invite him up?

"So…" Lex spoke, glancing up at my building with that trademark smirk of his returning. "I just got out of jail… Fancy a *fuck*?"

That accent… The words dripping off his lips… Yeah, I fancied it just fine, but I couldn't go through with it. Not like this.

Maybe he's not so changed after all.

"No," I answered, unsure whether or not I believed the word as it came out of my mouth.

I turned my back on him, ascending the stairs to my apartment building. Half of me expected him to grab my wrist – and I'd snap at him over it, but maybe, just *maybe*, I'd let him pull me into a furious embrace and breath the fire in my lungs...

As I turned behind the door, I saw one last glimpse of Alexander Lambert. He stood at the edge of the curb, staring at me like a broken man. We made eye contact for a fraction of a second before the door fell shut.

Chapter 14

Lex

Two days later, I stepped off of an airplane into the Heathrow International, crushed beyond recognition. I looked like such a mess that, even with just a thin hoodie and a pair of sunglasses, *nobody* recognized me as I navigated towards a taxi and back home.

It had all come crashing down around me.

Riley Ricketts was gone.

The Patrovo sponsorship was gone.

My rival Alistair Pritch had won.

All that I had left was Jess, and she was absolutely furious with me for fucking things up so badly. She barely spoke to me on the flight back, electing to get into a separate taxi and head back for her small countryside cottage.

In truth, I barely had *her* at all.

Three hours of traffic and drizzling rain later, my driver pulled up to the gates outside my lavish home. He finally realized with one look at the house that I was loaded, but still couldn't seem to place me.

"You some kind of big deal, brother?"

"Not anymore," I told him, slipping a substantial tip into his hand. "Not anymore..."

I realized that he was ignoring my words – mostly because his eyes were too busy counting the bills I'd handed him. He glanced back up at the gate, and the driveway that stretched beyond it. "You want me to take you up to the door? Looks like quite a walk."

"Absolutely not," I told him, pulling the hood up as the dismal rain rose in volume. I closed the door and let myself through a side gate, and then carried my suitcase up the lonely, sluggish route to the front of my small mansion.

Lambert House was priceless, mostly due to the sheer size of the property and the thick virtually impregnable wall surrounding it. It had belonged to a Duke of some nature, living out here in the countryside. A summer getaway spot for royalty...

I called it home.

My eyes scanned the windows in the distance as my shoes sloshed through the mud. Even with all this pea gravel, it did barely anything to hold back the natural consequences of consistent rainfall.

Chet, my groundskeeper, was sailing towards me in his little covered cart, maneuvering around thick puddles and loose, soggy earth to skitter to a stop near me.

"Mister Lambert! This is no weather to be taking a walk, good sir! Let me take you inside!"

I nodded, although I doubted he noticed the gesture in the rain. Instead, I lugged my suitcase onto the back tray of his cart beneath the canvas bonnet of the vehicle, and took a soaked seat in the passenger's chair. He took one forlorn look at me before driving us towards the manor steps.

"Permission to speak freely?" He asked.

"Granted."

"Mister Lambert, I'm afraid that you look positively dreadful."

I laughed heartily to myself, naturally alarming him. After I wiped away the uncomfortable, dripping rain from my face, I commented: "Let's just say I've had a rough couple of days."

He kept his eyes forward, carefully whizzing us through patches of solid ground. "I take it that America didn't treat you kindly, then?"

"My trip was… complicated."

"Ah, I see."

Of course, he didn't really. But the sympathy was appreciated, and we sat in silence for the last three minutes of the drive.

Once I'd pulled myself indoors, a maid brought me a towel and took my suitcase up to my main bedroom. There were only a few members on my staff, but they acted quickly and diligently at my appearance, already having some arrangements made as soon as I appeared within the gates.

A fresh change of clothes – my usual business attire – was ready for me in the foyer. I wasn't particularly feeling myself, so I left them where they were and wandered upstairs, changing into something a little more casual.

My staff sensed the change in my demeanor, and gave me a wide berth as I settled back home. It only occurred to me a few hours later that they were likely expecting my publicist to have joined me for the trek, and so I knew that they realized things were amiss.

Behind the manor, I had contracted the installation of an enclosed football field. Since the rain had done absolutely nothing to let up, I took the accompanying underground passage out to the field. It was less than half a kilometer of walking, and it was blissfully dry. When I arrived, I switched on the industrial lighting and marveled at how the water roared against the glass ceiling and walls before retrieving the best looking football from my equipment room.

It was time to work a few things out the only way I knew how.

I spent well over an hour kicking the ball around, fighting imaginary opponents on the field. I remembered my first year of owning this place, I'd invite friends over for garden parties before taking on any and all challengers in the diminutive glass stadium.

But now, there was just me.

My arrival was less conspicuous than I had imagined. I was surprised to hear a buzzing as I knocked the football into the opposite goal once again, claiming another imaginary victory against my perceived opponents. Turning and panting, I spotted a small assortment of people on the opposite wall, shaking off umbrellas and standing in the covered foyer room outside.

Jogging over towards them, I realized that it was my usual group of friendly competitors – some amateur players from my schooling days, most of my National team, and a couple of members of the staff who were avid football fans and players.

There were a little less than two dozen of them… just enough to play a game. Jess must have been working a little magic. Maybe she hadn't given up on me yet…

"What are you lot doing here?" I asked as I unlocked the entrance and let them all in. They hung their wet jackets in the nearby coatroom, smiling and clasping my hand in turn.

"What, you're gonna come back and not tell us?" Jarvis MacNeil grinned, gripping me by the shoulder. He was one of the defenders on my team, and a rigorous force to deal with.

"My mind's been a little preoccupied the last few days," I confessed.

"Well, I can certainly see that!" Another chimed in. This one was Kil Humapoor, an old dormitory mate who had the gift, but was just too lazy to audition for teams. "You head straight onto the field to play alone after a sudden flight back? Not a person here that doesn't know that means something's wrong, man."

"I don't want to talk about it," I muttered.

"No need to talk with words, bro," Jarvis replied. "Do it with your feet. Let's dance!"

The twenty of them changed into athletic attire in the equipment rooms. Afterwards, we split into two teams and set the stage for our match beneath the storm.

With Humapoor electing to play as referee to maintain the balance, we chose our sides and set the green battlefield for war. Above us, the rain pounded against the glass as we fought valiantly for the ball. The storm's intensity was cheering us on.

Both teams were short a man, but we were able to work around that mutual handicap. I took my usual position as an offensive striker, dominating the ball and barking orders to my team as I led a vicious charge against the others.

Jarvis MacNeil had been nominated as captain of the opposition, and took a conservative, defensive approach. After years of playing together, he knew my weaknesses, and was able to hold us back time and time again… but he wasn't prepared for the level of frustration and bitterness that I brought to the green.

I ran faster than ever.

My kicks were stronger than ever.

Fueled by hate and animosity, I channeled every last ounce of my blinding fury into my plays, unafraid to test the patience of our ref and to lash out if it meant gaining additional ground, crippling a tactical advantage of the opposing team, or smiting down one of their brief shots at temporary victory.

During a break, MacNeil and Humapoor approached me, tossing me a bottle of water as they downed their own.

"Dude, what the fuck is the matter with you?" MacNeil asked, giving me a fierce look as I squeezed the bottle into my mouth. "You're playing like a wild fucking animal."

"Nothing's the matter," I insisted gravely.

"You're acting possessed out there, dude," Humapoor added. "I've never seen you so unchained on the green. It's like you're on the *bloody* attack!"

"I *said,* everything is *fine*," I hissed, letting my insipid glare fuel the emotion.

"What the hell happened in America?" He pressed me, simultaneously pushing his luck as well as my buttons.

I stood up from the bench, putting my nose inches from his as I glared him down. "It's done. It's finished. What happened there is *over.* And now I have to *deal* with that."

"You're *Lightning Lex,*" MacNeil kicked in, stepping up to back up our friend. While MacNeil hadn't encountered him during school, they'd gained a healthy respect for each other during our impromptu matches, and bonded over a shared love of premium cigars. "Whatever happened, you can fix it."

"What part of *it's over* didn't you quite understand?" I snarled at him.

"The part where you got back on a plane like a yellow-bellied coward instead of taking care of your fucking business," MacNeil spat back, fueling me into a rage. "I don't know what's got you set off, but I know it has nothing to do with the story in the rags. You want to hide away in your glass cage and beat the piss out of a ball? That's your problem. You start taking it out on your friends during a friendly match? Ain't fucking *nothing* friendly about what you're doing out here. Either tone your shit down and accept whatever your fuck-up is, or get back out there and take care of your shit."

I wanted to deck him, but I knew the others would be on me in a second. Of course, he made a compelling point.

I *was* Lighting Lex Lambert.

What the fuck was I doing out here?

"*That's* the Lex I remember," Humapoor told me, staring into my eyes. "Now, get back out here and show us all how a World Cup player *really* does it."

That's exactly what I did.

I played with precision, careful calculation, and tactical dominance. Instead of leading a crushing vendetta against the other team, I hung back, guiding the others towards victory, playing support and taking charge when the ranks broke or ownership if the ball became too ambiguous to my tastes.

This half of the game, we won by a devastating six goals.

Once we'd washed up in the showers and changed back into our regular clothes, I realized that the weather was finally letting up. I walked with them across the grounds instead of taking the underground passage, watching how the recent rainfall glistened off of the foliage and flora of my gardens.

I invited them all inside and requested that the staff put all hands on deck to whip up a small feast for us. I brought out some home-baked snacks to keep everyone satiated for the time being, and left them in the main gaming room to play pool, watch the big screen, toss darts, and help themselves to my liquor cabinet and bar.

"Aren't you joining us?" One of the others asked as I turned to make my leave.

"I'll be back in a short while, gentlemen," I smiled. "I have a couple of affairs that demand my immediate attention… please, make yourselves comfortable until I return."

I left them to their devices as I strolled down to the privacy of my foyer, whipping out my cell phone and dialing Jess.

She answered on the third ring.

"What do you want?"

I ignored the aggravation in her tone.

"Jess, I need to apologize for my behavior the last few days," I told her. "I lost my cool in New Orleans… I know you meant the best for me and I'm sorry I cocked it all up. What you did here… Getting the guys together… I needed this."

"Don't mention it you damned fool. I've already forgiven you," Jess chuckled. "Glad to see you came to your senses so quickly. I thought you might hole yourself up in your little stadium and play football for a week before *anyone* saw you again."

"I might still take a couple more hours," I smiled.

She laughed down the line.

"So come out with it. I know you didn't just call me to say thanks."

"Did you find the number I'm looking for?" I asked.

"You pay me for a reason, don't you?" Jess laughed. "Of course I have the damn number."

"In that case, put me through to Gloria Van Lark…"

Chapter 15
Riley

When I came back down to the Pulliam Gallery, I had no idea what awaited me. It wasn't every day the head curator summoned me down to speak with a possible buyer, and some of my largest and most expensive works were housed in the Pulliam… I was completely taken aback by whom my mystery admirer was.

"Oh, it's you again," I smiled at the lithe, old woman. She was dressed in a long, oversized coat and loafers, carefully regarding one of my biggest paintings. This one carried a price tag higher than most automobiles, and I never would have assumed she could have afforded it… "How are you doing?" I asked quietly.

"I'm a bit cold, but I think I'll manage," she responded warmly as I walked up. Her eyes remained on the artwork. "You know, most artists these days feel like they have to be so self-important… that they must reinvent the wheel… bring something completely new to the field. In some cases, it's true. Most who try, fail. But you… I've given it some thought. I think you have some serious talent for your craft."

I glanced nostalgically up at the painting.

"What do you think of it?" I asked.

"You're asking for my opinion?"

"I am," I nodded. "I have my personal thoughts on it, but I wonder what you think. You were so kind to me last time, after all."

The old woman turned to the canvas and sighed to herself, contemplating the presentation. This wasn't one of my usual landscapes – it was the painting of a small girl, holding a puppy upright in her arms as she stood along the beach, its legs dangling down. Her back was to the water, and her pet covered most of her smiling face. The tide was nipping at her ankles as she faced the viewer, and the sun was setting quietly in the background.

"Fear," she finally spoke.

"Fear? What do you mean by that?"

The woman glanced over at me tenderly, and then back to the painting again. "See how the child faces away from the ocean? She has turned her back on the world, hiding behind the comfort of another living creature. She feels the cold of the tide, but refuses to venture into its embrace. This child is one who is trapped between worlds – unable to join that of the spectator, and unwilling to exist joyously within her own."

"That's an interesting conclusion," I remarked, pressing a pair of fingers to my chin as I studied the artwork alongside her. "I'd always thought it more of the opposite – refusing the comfort of the sea to confront the audience, offering up the sight of the dog as a gift, maybe."

The woman smiled. "Such is the wonder of art. Such varied interpretations. You never know what the artist expects or the audience finds."

"Do you like it?" I asked her curiously.

"Yes, I believe that I do. I'm somewhat fond of the artist herself, having been able to converse with her a few times."

"I painted this one," I responded, confused. "I've only seen you here twice now."

"I know," she winked. "But I've been here a little more often than that. You just haven't seen me... but I've seen you. And I've spoken to you, through observing your artwork. You are an interesting young woman, Riley."

"I don't believe I've ever gotten your name," I recalled, reaching out my hand to her. "You obviously know who I am. Riley Ricketts. Who might you be?"

"Oh, you know who I am," she smiled. "You've been waiting for me for a long time."

The cogs in my brain snapped, trying to rectify this impossible scenario. It couldn't be. But it was...

"You're Gloria Van Lark," I murmured.

She smiled triumphantly. "Indeed."

My brain worked at a hundred miles an hour. "But... your reputation... you're supposed to be tall, hawkish, with dark hair and spectacles... I've seen pictures of you! I've *met* you!"

Gloria smiled knowingly. "My proxy, Paulette. She operates in my stead, representing me across the world. I have taught her over the many years to reflect my precise eye for artwork, and I sometimes accompany her to ensure that the proper decisions are made."

"So, that was Paulette that I spoke with before."

"Aye," Gloria acknowledged. "I stayed in town for a few days, enjoying some of your delicious cuisine and museums. I wasn't sold on your work, but a very compelling phone call convinced me to give you another try."

"Phone call?"

"Your investor," she clarified. "On principle, I would have turned the money down, but I was nonetheless intrigued by his offer…"

"I don't know what *investor* you might be talking about, but I'm glad to have had the opportunity to meet you – *properly*, this time," I found myself blurting out.

"Agreed. You say you don't know who it is?"

"Not at all," I answered truthfully.

She stepped closer, peering deeply into my eyes. I felt a strong sense of sudden invasion as she glanced into the windows to my soul, studying me very, very carefully.

"...I see," she murmured to herself. "Well, that convinces me then."

"Convinces you of what?" I asked, unwilling to let my hopes rise too much.

"I wanted to be the one to tell you to your face that Gloria Van Lark *cannot* be bought. Not with fancy words, and not with million dollar donations."

Million dollar donations? Lex! What the hell did you do?!?

"But I can see now that you haven't orchestrated this meeting... And... Perhaps I've grown rather fond of a *few* of your pieces during my time here in New Orleans."

I hung on her every word, and Gloria beamed with pride as she spoke the words I never thought I'd hear in my wildest dreams:

"Riley Ricketts, I would be my pleasure to purchase select pieces to feature in your very own exhibit within the *Spinnoc* galleries."

I could barely contain my excitement.

"Oh, thank you! Thank you so much!" I exclaimed, resisting every urge to throw my arms around this woman and hug her to death. "This means so much to me... I can't possibly thank you enough…"

"There is a condition," she added quickly.

"A condition?" I asked, puzzled at her tone.

"Walk with me," Gloria told me, and I fell into step beside her as we crossed the museum, passively observing the exhibits.

"The condition is your undivided attention," she stipulated. "I don't fancy *all* of your artwork, but I do appreciate a few choice selections. If you want an exhibit in the *Spinnoc*, you will have to focus entirely on your craft. You will need to move to San Diego. I can give you room and board with studio access, and I'll fully expect to see more of your work within several months."

"Move to San Diego? I…."

Gloria cut me off before I could finish my thought.

"And I want none of these landscapes. They're good, but not nearly good enough to display in my galleries. Leave them to the professionals, and concentrate on the conceptual pieces and portraits that really demonstrate your talent."

"You... want me to move across the country?"

"Well, naturally," she answered, glancing over at me. "That won't be a problem, will it?"

"I'll... have to think about that," I answered. "I mean, my whole life is here. For a short while, I thought about going to England with someone, but we had a bit of a... *falling out*. He left the country a couple of days ago."

"England, you say?" She commented. "Well. That certainly makes sense. It seems you may know your investor after all..." she eyed me sideways, "...or you only just figured that out. Either way, you should have probably reconciled with him when you had the chance."

"Why's that?"

"I thought he perhaps loved you. I could hear it in his voice as we spoke. He must have divested a great deal of resources into finding me, because I make myself scarce on purpose… and I don't particularly enjoy being found."

I had no response. I just turned and stared at the painting of the girl.

"Never mind all that," Gloria continued. "I can see I was mistaken as to the strength of your relationship… If you wish to pursue proper representation in my galleries, you will accompany me back to California. The last thing I need is for you to become distracted with such *mundane* affairs when I've come to recognize your worth."

"When do you need a decision?" I asked quietly, thinking about Lex. Why had he done this? I'd shut him out of my life. Did he think bribing Gloria would win me over?

Gloria glanced at a modest watch on her arm. "You have approximately fourteen hours before we board my private jet back to California. I trust that you'll pack light. I can make the arrangements to observe and purchase any of your existing artwork that I see fit to obtain, but I'll be expecting you to settle yourself quickly and get straight to work. No dilly-dallying."

I thought to my life here in New Orleans, and how rooted I was in this magnificent city. My soul had flourished here for years, powered by the magic in this place.

And then there were my friends.

Reiko would understand, but she'd hate it. She was such a fantastic companion that I dreaded being separated from her. I knew she hated California and wouldn't be willing to move out that way for me.

Will would be devastated. Sure, he could be a pain in the ass, but he was a valuable friend and had been a strong component to my support network since we were kids. Over the last few days we'd reconciled, and I think he finally understood the way our relationship needed to be... But leaving on such sudden notice would be hard...

"As I said, you have fourteen hours," Gloria Van Lark repeated, turning on her heel. "If you wish to accompany me, you will meet me here at the steps to this museum at that time. I eagerly await your answer."

With that, the mysterious curator of one of the world's most prestigious and exclusive museums turned on a heel, strolling straight towards the exit.

I felt like I was going to topple to the ground. This was no ordinary offer. I reached out behind myself as my knees began to buckle. My fingertips found a bench, and I collapsed down into it, struggling to process everything that just happened.

I had a choice to make:

My dream, finally come true?

Staying here with my friends and my life?

And what the hell was I going to do about Lex?

I had less than a day to decide… and I didn't have the faintest idea of what to do.

Chapter 16
Lex

I was standing on the upper floor, staring out over the grounds, when the phone rang in my pocket. I checked the caller ID… and almost dropped it to the floor when I realized who was on the line.

Staring at the name for a moment, I accepted the call and lifted the receiver to my ear. "I didn't expect to hear from you again."

"I just met Gloria Van Lark," Riley blurted breathlessly into the phone.

"Oh, did you?" I responded thoughtfully.

"Yeah." She sounded on edge.

"Well… how did that go?"

"Turns out that she likes me, and apparently wants to represent me in her museum," Riley responded. "No thanks to my *investor*!"

"An investor, huh?" I asked, measuring my words carefully. "Didn't know that you had yourself one of those."

"Cut the shit, Lex," she finally snapped. "You tried to pay her off. She came to the museum to tell me I couldn't buy her!"

"Well it sounds like you worked through that… I *knew* you would, Riley." I replied, smirking into the phone.

"Wait a second… You knew? You knew what?"

"Gloria Van Lark is piece of work Riley. She can't be bought," I said.

"Then why did you try to buy her?!? Did you seriously give her museum a million freaking dollars?" Riley shouted over the line.

"I did it because I knew that was the only way she would see you *personally*. I did my research at great personal expense. Gloria likes to hide behind her staff and she never gives *anyone* a second chance… But she lives for the opportunity to crush someone's dreams."

"You manipulated her?" Riley asked, incredulous. "You knew she'd come to tell me off?"

"It was worth a shot," I commented. "So, what happens now?"

"Now?" Riley sounded pensive. "Like I said, she wants to represent me... but she expects me to move to California with her."

"I see," I remarked. "Are you going to do it."

"I have no idea," Riley confided. "It's a dream come true to be offered representation, and I can barely fathom how much she's considering paying for my art... but it's a lot to ask of me."

"Right."

"You didn't have to do this, Lex."

"I know that. But I wanted to just express some... *regret* over how things happened. I know that you're moving on, but I wanted you to understand that I'm sorry."

"I'm sorry too," Riley whispered down the line. "I was being selfish... Thinks were just moving too fast... I should have been there for you. I shouldn't have... left you. And now you're gone."

"I miss you," I quickly blurted out, unwilling to talk myself out of expressing the sentiment. "I wish you were here."

Riley remained quiet on the line.

"...Riley?"

Finally, she responded: "Oh god, Lex, I've made a huge mistake. I miss you too."

I closed my eyes and rested my face against the window, holding the phone pressed against my ear. "I want you here, Riley. I haven't stopped thinking about you since we parted ways... and I've been a wreck. Losing you devastated me... and I know I can't have you, but I want you so badly."

There was another piercing silence over the phone. I feared with every passing second that I would hear the line disconnect.

In fact, I thought it did briefly, but that's when I noticed Jess trying to dial me on the other line. I ignored her call and continued to hold out for Riley's response.

"If I don't go to San Diego... I'm walking away from the opportunity of a lifetime."

"You never needed Gloria before, and you don't need her today. If you want to go, you should go. Maybe I can visit next time I'm in the states..."

Another piercing silence… punctuated by the sound of soft crying. Concern clouded my thoughts, and I felt my heart quiver with pain.

"Riley?"

"I love you, Lex."

It was my turn to be stunned.

"…I love you too, Riley."

"I can't do this."

"What can't you do?"

"I can't take her offer. She wants me to forsake any distractions…"

"Why is that a problem?" I asked.

"Because you're a distraction. You're a big goddamned distraction!" Riley shouted.

"That was her condition: move to California and give up *everything* else. Focus only on my artwork. She thinks that I need to work under a different atmosphere and to give up my life in order to produce my best work. She's only giving me fourteen hours to decide, and then I'm gone…"

The phone buzzed against my ear again.

It was Jess again.

I ignored the call.

"Riley... you *have* to take this chance," I insisted. "You've worked so hard for this opportunity. All I could do was get her to listen to you. You *have* your chance. You've got to take it."

"I don't care about that anymore," she whispered sadly down the phone. "I never told you this... But... The magic came back."

"The magic?" I thought aloud. "You mean, your art? You're satisfied with your painting again?"

"I am," she told me confidently. "After we met, I painted something... I haven't shown it to anyone yet. It's different... It's better. Being with you made me better."

She wasn't the only one... Jess had been right. Riley was the best thing that ever happened to me...

"I don't need to be in some stuffy San Diego studio... I need to be with you. You bring out my best creative side. You made me so happy, even if I wasn't willing to admit it to myself... or to you."

"So, what do you want to do, then?" I asked. The silence was deafening. I could feel the conflict through the line.

"Lex… I don't know what to do," she whispered.

"I'm coming back Riley. I'll be on a plane tonight. Whatever decision you make tomorrow, I want to be there…"

This was more than I could have ever hoped for. I practically hurled a victory fist into the sky.

"Gloria Van Lark expects an answer from me around mid-afternoon… can you get here before then?"

"I'll be there for you," I reassured her.

"Thank you, Lex…"

I could barely contain myself as I hung up the phone, but before I had a chance to celebrate, it was ringing again.

Jess… Shit…

"I was on the other line," I explained with a small grin as I answered the call. "I have news for you. Are you ready?"

"You're not the only one," she replied, sounding incredibly enthusiastic. "Who is the best fucking publicist in the world?"

"I'm going to guess *you*," I replied.

For some reason, something felt amiss.

"I expect more conviction in your voice the next time I ask that question, buddy," Jess chuckled. "Better put on your best fucking suit because I'm already on my way. I'm going to be there in an hour."

"What, why? I'm heading out the door. I've got a plane to catch."

"No, you *definitely* don't," she chided me. "Not when you hear *this* news: Lex Lambert, you've officially landed a direct meeting with the Head of Public Relations for the Patrovo Corporation himself. Cancel whatever you were about to do, because no matter *what* it was… it can wait."

"…Brett Barker wants to see me?"

"You're goddamn right he does."

The phenomenally bad timing clicked in my head, and I groaned as my forehead braced against the window again. My view incorporated the enclosed glass stadium, the various gardens, and a river that ran across the estate… but my eyes focused on the stadium, cruelly mocking me.

"…Lex, are you there?"

"I'm here," I sighed.

"You sound a lot less enthusiastic about this than you should be. I know that you're beating yourself up over Riley, but c'mon. You've been waiting for this for ages."

"Why does he want to see me *now?*"

Jess's tone grew agitated. "Because it's the only time I could work you in, unless you planned on waiting a week. By then, the decision would be made."

"I don't get it. I thought he was adamantly against offering me the sponsorship?"

"Well… it just so turns out that your little bar brawl was recorded. Joys of living in a time where everybody's got a cellphone camera. And guess who showed up on camera taunting you?"

"Alistair!"

"It's all over the tabloids. Alistair tries to get his own teammate arrested in the US. They have the whole thing on video. The guy attacking you, the way you tried to defend yourself, and Alistair acting like a damn fool. Barker won't touch the guy with a ten-foot pole," Jess said, laughing.

"That can't be enough to entertain the thought of offering me the sponsorship."

Jess grew hesitant. "…I might have gone a little further. There's some rumors that you defended a young, vulnerable woman from a sexual attack…"

"I told you not to use Riley!" I shouted angrily.

"And I didn't. The Patrovo Corporation asked me about it. Turns out somebody got their hands on a police report. That'll be front page news tomorrow. What was I going to do, lie?"

"I told you under absolutely *no circumstances* were you to exploit Riley's trauma to benefit me," I said, my anger still bubbling to the surface.

"And I made that very clear as well, which seemed to impress Brett Barker. Look, you can hate me all you want, but I've bought you your shot. He's willing to overlook the scandals and the attitude if you can convince him that you're turning over a new leaf... and your single rival has been taken out of the picture. He's left with you, or picking someone with half your personality and pop culture draw. All you have to do is come with me and meet him yourself."

"I can't go," I told her definitively. "Because–"

"The *hell* you can't," Jess snapped. "I don't give a *bloody sod* how mad you might be over this. I get it. You don't want to exploit the girl's trauma. Fine. But you've been working towards this for months. Everything you've done has been to secure this multi-million contract. I am *handing it to you on a silver fucking platter.* All you have to do is not fuck this up, yeah?"

"Jess."

"Do *not*. I'll be there in under an hour. We can be meeting Brett in two more. Just put on your best fucking suit and–"

"JESS!"

She instantly shut up, pausing to absorb the anger in my voice. While I composed myself briefly, a moment of tension crackled between us. "What?" She finally asked.

"I was on the phone with Riley when you were trying to call me earlier."

"Yeah, and…?"

Her tone changed. "…Oh."

"Yeah. *Oh.* Jess, we reconciled. She knows about the donation. Gloria Van Lark decided to take her in, but only if she moved to California and completely committed herself to the craft."

"Oh! That's the tits!"

"No, Jess," I groaned, pinching the bridge of my nose. "She doesn't want to do it. She wants to come back here – to England."

"This girl has it bad for you Lex," Jess laughed.

"Maybe. Point is, I just got done telling her I'm jumping on a plane. I want to be there before she has to make a decision with Gloria tomorrow…"

"Oh, *fuck me sideways*," Jess groaned.

"Exactly."

"Lex… there's no way I can reschedule this thing with Brett and Patrovo Corp. It's now or never. Can't Riley wait, just a couple of hours? You're already down a million this week on your little donation, and this is turning down an awful lot more… This is your dream!"

"I don't care about the fucking money or the goddamn contract anymore, Jess."

I realized that I'd said the words before I even recognized what they meant. I was stunned at how my heart had overrode my brain, sending a signal to blurt that declaration out… but even as I wondered about this, I knew that it was true.

All that mattered to me was Riley Ricketts.

"You really mean that, don't you, Lex?"

I didn't need to give it another second's thought. "I do, Jess. I really do."

"Well, I'll be absolutely damned," she laughed down the phone. "I thought this little trip might be a good idea upfront… give you some renewed perspective, keep you out of trouble… but you're a changed man, Alexander Lambert. This woman has really gotten into you."

"I think she has."

"Alright then," she exhaled, the tension leaving her tone. "In that case, fuck the contract. I'll make the call right after we disconnect. If he can't wait one more day to hell with the whole damn company. You get yourself to the airport. I'll call ahead and have a plane ready for you."

"You're the best, Jess," I told her, sighing out in relief. "I can't possibly thank you enough."

"Yeah, yeah," she chuckled. "Go get suited up and head straight for Heathrow. Hit me with a text when you land."

Chapter 17

Riley

There was just one other person I had to speak to.

To the world, she was one of the most talented contemporary sculptors of our time – someone whose highly sought work occupied exhibits in over a hundred museums across the world. Highly reclusive, barely conducting interviews anymore, word was that she had hidden herself away somewhere in the vast archipelago of islands beneath Greece.

Mom was always dramatic like that.

I hadn't spoken to Jolene Ricketts in years, and I still remembered the last conversation. Well, more accurately, the last vicious fight. We didn't exactly see eye to eye, but something told me that she was going to be indispensible to me as I really set this major crossroads into stone.

She picked up on the fourth try.

"Hullo? Margaret speaking," the weary voice on the other line spoke.

"Mom... it's me."

"…My stars, Riley?"

I suppressed a small smile at the sound of her confusion. "Yeah, it's Riley. It's been a long time."

"It's funny… I thought I might never hear from you again," she told me matter-of-factly. "I take it that you need something from me. Is it money?"

If people thought that Gloria Van Lark was stiff as a board, then they hadn't met my mother. It always surprised me how such an emotive and passionate sculptor could be such a cold, callous bitch to her own flesh and blood.

"I need advice."

"Advice," she chuckled. "Why on *earth* would you call me in the middle of the night for *advice?*"

Oh shit, I thought to myself. *I didn't bother to check for the time zone difference…*

"Because I need you, Mom," I answered plainly. "I'm sorry to call so late, I didn't notice the time… but if you can spare me a couple of minutes, I've got a problem that I think you can help me with."

She sighed briefly. "Fine. What is it?"

"I met Gloria Van Lark today."

The silence over the phone was deafening.

"Gloria Van Lark approached you? In the flesh? Describe her. How did she look? I need to know for certain."

"I met Paulette first, who matched the stories. But the real thing was an old woman in a disguise that I can only accurately call *homeless chic*."

"That's her, alright," Mom remarked. *Of course she knew the truth about Gloria... her work had probably been sitting in Spinnoc for a long time now.* "If Gloria came to see you, then maybe I was wrong about your painting … Did she at least make you an offer?"

"As much as I appreciate that stunning vote of confidence," I gritted my teeth, "Yes. She offered to purchase some of my artwork, so long as I packed up everything and returned with her to California. She's waiting for my final answer tomorrow."

"You mentioned a problem," Mom remarked. "I fail to see where it is, unless your problem is clawing for my attention while I'm trying to sleep."

It didn't surprise me that she failed to grasp the situation.

"Mom, I'm being torn three ways. New Orleans is magic to me. My friends are here. Everything that I know is here... San Diego is so far away... And then... There's Lex."

"Oh here we go," mother said, letting out a little laugh. "You know, I thought you grew out of boy troubles a long time ago?"

"Lex is trouble," I confirmed. "I have to choose between launching my career into the stratosphere, or being with one of the most visible celebrities in British culture."

"You're exaggerating."

"I'm not. Are you familiar at all with footba– I mean, with *soccer*?"

"It's not my thing," Mom replied, "although the locals go batshit insane over the sport. You're dating an English player? Who?"

"His name is Lex Lambert."

"...Son of a bitch."

My heart dropped. "Wait, what? What's the matter?"

Mom laughed down the phone. "*Lightning Lex Lambert*? He's one of the few I *do* recognize. His sticky thumb is in half of the scandals that come out of England... what on earth possessed you to chase *him?* He's going to dump you in a heartbeat!"

"He's changed, Mom," I told her, realizing how naïve I probably sounded to her.

"Hogwash. He's a renegade, Riley. Although, I'll admit that marrying him would set you up for life... Paintings or no paintings, that's the practical choice."

"I don't care about the money," I told her emphatically. "I can make it on my own... I just need to know that I'm not making a huge mistake."

"Choose Gloria," Mom answered. "It's the best decision I made in my entire life. Under her mentoring, your work will be known and appreciated the world over. I never regretted taking her up on the *same* offer..."

"Wait... what are you talking about?"

"Don't be daft, Riley. You're not the first Ricketts that drew the attention of Gloria Van Lark. No, she came to me about fifteen years ago, long after I'd established myself in the field. She told me that she could teach me to hone my craft to exceptional heights… and so she did." bookmark

"Mom… that's about the time that you left."

"Oh, I'm aware," she commented. "My art was everything to me, Riley. I made my choice and I don't regret it. Look at me now… I'm arguably the most distinguished and decorated sculptor living today."

"Mom, you… y-you *left* me? For… for *her?*" I stammered, barely able to acknowledge this sudden change in my understanding of things.

"When you put it that way, it makes me sound sort of rough, doesn't it?" She chuckled airily down the line. "I saw to it that your needs were met. Your foster parents were sent appropriate amounts of money to give you everything that you needed, and they showed me some of your art as you grew up. It wasn't too bad."

I could feel my phone shaking against my head. All this time… I had been dreaming of gaining the attention of Gloria Van Lark… and the bitch had had a hand in ruining my childhood from the start.

My mother had abandoned me, yes. I had known that a long time ago. She chose her career…

Gloria Van Lark had done what she does best… She crushed someone under foot.

She crushed me…

Abandon your life.

Leave all of this behind.

I'll make you world-famous.

I didn't even care what Mom was prattling on about anymore. I took a few deep breaths and returned to the conversation.

"…You'd be making a fool of yourself if you turned down this opportunity, not that you were ever particularly bright."

"I appreciate the help, Mom," I told her.

She went quiet.

"You're angry. Last time you got angry you didn't talk to me for six years…"

"Maybe I can set a new record," I replied, hanging up the line.

The phone clattered to the couch as I held my head in my hands and sobbed. The last couple of days had taken their toll on me, but I knew that I was making the right choice.

Fuck Gloria Van Lark, and fuck her museum. I'd come this far in life without her and I wasn't about to let her control my life.

With this sentiment in mind, I needed some paintbrush therapy. I'd already prepared the canvas with a thin veneer of clear. I leapt off of the couch and perched myself in front of my easel, whipping up a dozen colors and blends for my pallet.

The white frame sat before me, eagerly waiting for my touch. It called to me, showing me exactly what I needed to do.

I dabbed my brush against a soothing blue, moving a glob of it to a clean spot on my pallet. Mixing in a touch of white to deepen the variance, I pressed the tip to the canvas... and I performed my greatest composition yet.

A few hours later, I was putting the finishing touches on the canvas when the door clicked open. I allowed myself to slip back out of my zone as the telltale clatter of Reiko's boots navigated towards my studio, pausing at a few rooms.

There was someone else with her – Will, in all likelihood. Even *he* couldn't bother me now.

"Riley, I just want to apologize for the way I've been acting lately," I heard him call for me. "I know that it's not fair to you, and I swear that I'm okay with just being–"

The movements stopped at my doorway. I turned around, stepping away from my latest painting as I stretched before them.

"Holy shit," Reiko muttered.

"That is... wow," Connor murmured, pushing his glasses further up his nose. "I think this might be your best one yet."

"You think so?" I asked nonchalantly, pulling up a stool and taking a seat. I followed their collective gaze to the paint, still drying against the canvas. Glancing down at my own clothes, I could see abrupt dashes of color all over, a sea of smudges and splotches.

I must have been painting like a wild animal.

"I take it back," Connor continued. "I understand now. I thought the ones in the Closet of Doom were good, but *this… this* is on a completely different level."

"This is what I see… This is what I want to create..."

Reiko swallowed. "That Van Lark chick is going to *love* you."

"Oh, no she's not," I smiled knowingly. "Not when I'm through with her."

Reiko exchanged a quick, confused glance with Will, and then turned her attention back to me. "Wait, did we miss something? Because that lady's been all you could talk about for months."

I stood up, grasping both of them by the shoulder. I was careful to not smear any excess paint on either of them. "Order some delivery and crack open some beers, because I have so much to tell you guys…"

And I did.

I told them absolutely everything.

Every last detail about my relationship with Lex, the way we'd broken apart, meeting Gloria Van Lark, the conversations with Lex and my mother over the phone…

We conversed long into the night, and they both emphatically told me that they would support whatever decision I made.

My friends had my back.

And when I arrived at the steps of the Pulliam Museum, I had my definitive decision already in mind.

Even with no Lex Lambert in sight.

"Welcome back, Riley," Gloria chuckled as I stepped into earshot. "I see that you brought some friends. I'm afraid that they won't be able to join us… and what's this?"

She was referring to the covered painting under my arm. I'd protected it with my life all the way here, and I unsheathed it before her, balancing the bottom edge against the top of my sandal as I held the huge piece up.

"My… my gods," Gloria Van Lark murmured. Even Paulette's cold smirk dropped, and she adjusted her spectacles to gaze at the artwork. "When did *this* happen?"

"I painted this yesterday afternoon, after our discussion," I answered her.

Gloria composed herself, but was unable to wrench her eyes from the artwork. "This is magnificent, Riley. This is *exactly* the standard of art that I expect for my galleries. I can tell you right this moment that *Spinnoc* would benefit tremendously from including this piece… it would appear that my faith in you wasn't misplaced after all. Like mother like daughter… If you can emote creations on this level, then you have all the makings of an extraordinary painter."

"I appreciate the vote of confidence," I told her.

She finally tore her eyes free and smiled at me. "Well, Riley… traveling light, I take it? No matter. We have everything that you could possibly need at the Foundation. Why don't you go ahead and say your goodbyes to your associates here? We have a long flight ahead of us, and I'll need to secure proper handling for this piece."

"Actually, there's something I need to say first," I responded in the kindest voice I could muster.

"You'd better make it quick," Gloria remarked, checking her watch. "We're pressed for time. What is it, Riley?"

I thought back to every ounce of happiness that had ever happened to me – tender times with my foster parents, my friends, my time with Lex Lambert – and I summoned up the biggest, sincerest smile that had ever crossed my face, just as they peered over my shoulder.

"Fuck you."

Chapter 18
Lex

"Actually, there's something I need to say first," Riley told Gloria Van Lark as I walked up.

At least, I *assumed* that was actually her... I'd never seen the woman myself, but she did look like a rather self-assured, self-absorbed old woman.

Gloria checked her watch quickly, looking rather irritated. "You'd better make it quick. We're pressed for time. What is it, Riley?"

Riley paused, lost in thought for a moment. I had considered hanging back for a few minutes and watching how this played out, but the *aeroplane* delays had already made me late enough as it was...

I walked up to her side, and her friends – the skittish thin one, and her Japanese friend, Reiko – glanced over at me with hushed tones. I smiled with a finger to my lips, preparing to surprise her.

Sure, this was an interesting moment to choose, but I'd gotten there as quickly as I could, and I intended on supporting her when she–

"Fuck you."

My hand clasped onto her shoulder right then, and I froze out of complete confusion. *What the* hell *did she just say?*

Riley glanced up at me in equal surprise, and a large smile spread across her lips. "Lex," she murmured. "You came after all. I was so afraid you wouldn't make it."

Gloria Van Lark looked impassive at best, but the stoic woman at her side bristled in anger.

"Excuse me... what the *hell* did you just say to Madame Van Lark?" The woman indignantly requested, her eyes becoming two blackened pits of coal beneath her spectacles. "How *dare* you speak to her this way, you ungrateful, *impetulant* disgrace of a–"

"You ruined my childhood, you miserable old bitch," Riley turned to Gloria. "You offered this same fucking deal to my mother, and she took it... She walked straight out of my life forever."

"I helped your mother blossom," Gloria replied calmly. "She deserved to have her gifts recognized by the world.

She needed someone to guide her. She was weak and impressionable…"

Gloria tilted her head thoughtfully.

"I had no earthly idea that my pupil's progeny would grow to be such a talented and… dare I say it, *fierce* young woman," Gloria commented. "I would have approached you *years ago* if I'd had the faintest clue… We can certainly make up for lost time."

"You don't seem to get it," Riley told her. "I'm not going with you."

"Nonsense," Gloria rebutted. "You couldn't possibly throw away this opportunity. Without my representation, you'll be dust in the wind, child. I'll find and train another to fill the hole you would have occupied. You'll be cast aside to rot while a worthy inheritor to the art rises in your stead. You don't *truly* want that, do you?"

Riley crossed her arms. "I think I'll take my chances."

"She's a damned good painter," I chimed in. "With the right people behind her, she'll rise with or without you. If I can get *your* attention, then I think I can certainly draw the right sets of eyes across the art community, wouldn't you say?"

Riley smiled my way. "There are other curators at other world-renowned museums. I can certainly knock on other doors."

"Not if those doors remain closed to you," Gloria Van Lark replied. "I can personally see to it that you are locked out of every reputable museum in the world. You'll struggle to have your art displayed in anything more elegant than a cheap motel lobby."

"Is that a threat?" Reiko chimed in.

"Absolutely," the old hag replied. "I suggest that you take the opportunity while it remains available… or else I will *end* your career, right here and now."

"You miserable old fuck," her other friend responded – what was his name, *Will?* "You would go out of your way to destroy an artist just because she turned down the chance to be *forced* into abandoning her life to come live under your thumb? You're not asking her to sell you some art – you want her to give up *everything* and come stay with you for, what, how long?"

"A decade, bare minimum," Gloria replied without a moment's hesitation. "Perhaps even two, given her age. It really depends on her stamina. You'll be able to paint round the clock with zero distractions…"

"I will absolutely *not* join you," Riley told her in the darkest tone of voice I'd ever heard out of her. "You are a wicked, *evil* woman, preying on young artists dreams and locking them away from the world… but *how? How* has nobody come out against you yet?"

"Nobody who has ever been offered my representation has turned me down. I'm offering you something beyond simple measure. A future you can only begin to imagine."

"Then call me the first," Riley replied. "The first to turn you down."

Gloria Van Lark and her proxy exchanged a meaningful glance, and then turned back to regard us coolly.

"Very well then, Riley," the elderly woman responded. "You are lucky that I'm booked throughout the rest of the year… but I *highly* suggest that you make the wisest use of your time for the next five months. Find a new field.

I'm afraid painting isn't in your future…"

"Get out of my fucking sight, you miserable old fuck," Riley smirked.

"Charming," Gloria answered, descending down the steps between us. She paused to look Riley hard in the eyes.

"You have searched for me for so long, haven't you? Many artists have, and many will continue to do so for years to come. I am afraid, my dear Riley, that you will come to regret this day."

Riley didn't say a word, and so the two of them stepped into a taxi and left the scene.

"Well… *that* was tense," Connor replied with a half-hearted chuckle. "Jesus. What a complete cunt…" he turned to Riley. "What are you going to do now?"

"I have absolutely no idea," she muttered. "I'll figure something out."

"So, what's that?" I asked Riley, indicating the covered canvas that she was holding close to her chest. "I haven't seen that since I walked up…"

Riley looked embarrassed for a moment, but revealed the painting to me.

I was completely taken aback.

"It's… it's…"

"It's you," she quietly told me.

The painting was unmistakably me. It was a portrait of me striking a football with my ankle, volleying around a player who dared to try to stop me. I was dressed in my Manchester United attire, from several years back…

It was the proudest game of my life.

"I looked you up, finally," Riley offered. "I searched for the highlights of your career. This game looked like the one that the British public loved the most, and one particular moment near the end…"

"I remember it fondly," I told her, feeling my chest swell with pride. "This moment happened in the last fifteen seconds of the game. It's right when I scored the winning point and led us to a close but decisive victory… and it's the game that finally put me on the road to the National team."

She smiled softly. "It's for you."

"I love it, Riley," I whispered, pulling her up into my arms and planting a firm kiss on her lips. When we pulled away, my eyes were full of love, and my heart was burning with passion for this wonderful, amazing woman. "And I love *you*."

"I love you too, Lex."

The other two shared a meaningful glance. Reiko stood a little closer to Connor as they turned away to allow us the moment.

I pressed my lips to her crown as I remembered one important detail…

I reached into my pocket and removed my phone, holding it up to the light. With a flick of my thumb against the screen, the microphone app stopped, and I saved the recording as *Gloria Van Lark, Evidence.*

"I need to make a quick phone call," I told her, kissing Riley on the cheek. "Can you wait here for a moment?"

"Absolutely," she groaned, sitting down on the stairs. "I don't think I have the energy to do much of anything else right now…"

"I'll be right back," I smiled reassuringly.

Wandering away from the group, I stepped over to a nearby column and pulled up my contacts. Within a few moments, I had Jess on the line.

"Lex! How did it go?"

"It was… not quite what I expected," I commented dryly. "Listen, I have something fascinating to share with you."

"Oh yeah? Whatcha got?"

"An opportunity," I smiled. "It would appear that Gloria Van Lark has a thing for scooping up promising young artists and giving them a classic case of Stockholm syndrome…"

"What?" She exclaimed. "No kidding!"

"Yes… I was intending to record Riley's big moment in accepting Gloria's deal, but what I wound up with is…" I paused, choosing my words carefully, "far more interesting.

"Jess, you're one of the most talented publicists I've ever heard of, and you've sharpened your teeth on keeping my nose clean in the eyes of the British public. You're skilled at representing me… and I don't know a soul who could do a better job than you."

"You flatter me," she replied warmly.

I could practically hear her smirk across the phone line as she anticipated my next words:

"I'm offering you a chance to do the complete opposite… how would you like to help me take down the most legendary art curator in the world?"

Chapter 19
Riley

When Lex told me what he had in mind, the only thing I wanted to do was drag him to my bed, rip all of his clothes off, and make love to him.

So that's exactly what I did.

His strong, powerful hands slid along my thighs as he left a trail of kisses along them, working his way towards my sex. Instead of stopping there, he lifted his lips to press against my stomach, tenderly caressing the area.

I slipped my fingers into his hair as he continued to worship my skin, licking a curving trail up towards my chest. My nipples, so recently pleased by his lips, stood just as erect as ever as he took one into his mouth with a satisfying smack of his lips.

"Oh god, Lex," I murmured with satisfaction as he boldly maintained eye contact with my half-lidded gaze.

I squirmed beneath his touch as he continued to ply my body with pleasure. His tongue deftly stroked my puckered nub, the teeth grazing lightly and tugging at the tiny, pink peak. I held his head close as he pleased me, every last lap of his tongue against my nipple causing a new shudder in my mind…

His palm squeezed against my other breast, the fingers outstretching across the supple flesh. He pinched the other nipple between his digits, rolling it slowly, tugging upward, and I exhaled a surprising little moan.

"You like that, hmm?" He asked confidently, already knowing the answer as he released my peak from his teeth.

"Mm-hmm," I nodded quietly.

"Not very convincing," he grinned wickedly, before diving back down to slip his mouth over my breast, sucking in my nipple once again. I felt his tongue gliding across the peak and moaned with delight, my arms squeezing his face down against my flesh even tighter.

He pulled back afterwards, running his fingernails down my sides as his face disappeared between my knees.

"Much better," I heard him chuckle, before he shouldered my thighs and lunged down towards my sex.

"Lex… *fuck*…"

His soft, cocky chuckle rolled over my exposed, wet pussy as his tongue married itself into my folds. I valiantly tried to keep my hips down against the sheets, but his deft maneuvers were too *tastefully* sinful for me to maintain my composure for long.

With my fingers wrapped in his hair, my palms pressing down against his head, I coerced him to burrow down deeper. Lex's fingertips dug into the flesh of my thighs as he held them braced around his head, pinching into my skin and eliciting only more rapturous moans from my lips.

"You are *way* too good at this," I sighed contently between mindless moans.

He only chuckled again, lifting his face just enough to slip his tongue against my aching clit.

I felt my body quiver with delight. The pressure was so good, and he was *so* great at what he was doing…

Mindlessly, I released my grip on his hair, clutching at my breasts, or the bedding, or whatever I could get my hands on. I alternated, clenching onto anything that would help me writhe in pleasure beneath the expert flicking of his wet, stiffened tongue.

Lex varied the movements and pressures against the bead of my passion, finally slipping away to kiss along the insides of my thighs again. I yearned for more, *needed* more, but he knew just how much teasing I really needed…

And that's when he grabbed my legs and effortlessly pulled me down the bed towards him, his eyes wild with lust.

"I need you, Riley," he murmured huskily as he planted the head of his cock against the lips of my wet, hungry pussy. "I need you so badly…"

"I need you too, Lex," I nodded with primal, lustful intent. "Please, just fuck me…"

He rolled the crimson head along the lips, exciting my nerve endings but unwilling to push in where I needed him. All the while, he kept his sexy half-smirk across his lips, one eyebrow rising to mock me.

"Dammit, you're such a tease…" I groaned.

"Only because I know you love it." He winked, holding his massive scepter still against my sex, daring me with his eyes to argue.

"Oh god, do I…"

Before I could register the movement, he was pushing deep into my chasm now, his huge cock eagerly taking ground deep within me. I was already starting to adjust to his mammoth size from our weeks of sexual encounters, and I was able to take more of him in on the first go…

"Oh *fuck*, Lex… god, I can't believe you haven't already torn me apart…"

"Honestly, I can't either," he grinned mischievously, but his own lustful gaze told me that his mind was already starting to melt with feral, animalistic need.

He wouldn't be coherent for long.

Then again… neither would I.

His hands clenched down onto my shoulders, pinning me beneath him as he slowly rocked his hips against mine. I knew how to relax myself against him now, letting in another inch with each wet, tender thrust, until he was finally hilting himself against my pelvis.

"Like a glove," I murmured softly.

"Like an *oven*," he groaned in correction.

His clear, wanton satisfaction only spurred me on, and I felt my arousal reach new, incredible peaks. I was now meeting his rolling hips with gusto, craving his flesh against mine and his body within my own more and more…

Lex growled with electric, crushing bliss as he rocked against me, his body dropping to steady itself against my own, but not heavy enough to crush it. He supported himself on one elbow as he pressed a palm against the headboard, keeping me trapped beneath his mighty, rippling muscles.

I loved the weight and the pressure. Just enough to let me easily breathe, but not enough to crush or discomfort me.

My hands rolled down his back, fingernails scratching down into the flesh. His lustful groan of approval only spurred me on, and I slipped my ankles over his calves and clutched onto this magnificent, sexy man with every drop of strength in my body.

…Well, until his penetrating thrusts drove me wild a little too long, and I felt the building pressure of an incredible orgasm. My moans evolved into something greater, something feral, as I clenched against his body and felt every inch of me seize up in anticipation.

"Oh god, just like that," I begged. "Harder. Faster. Please, Lex, don't stop… don't… *don't*…"

As the blinding climax struck my mind and released every ounce of tension within my body, I came with enough force to knock the wind out of my body.

Lex slowed for a moment, taking the instance to regain his breath as I sank down into the bedding in complete elation. Before I could get too comfortable, though, he was swinging me around onto my knees, facing away from him.

"Ooh... a bit rough, are we?"

He growled in my ear, nipping the lobe and earning a shudder down my spine. As he prepared to mount me from behind, I placed my palms against the headboard, throwing him a sexy little lip-bite over my shoulder.

"Take me, Lex," I murmured. "Take me now."

That's all the guidance he needed.

I felt his cock thrust deep into my soaked, ready pussy, and I bit down to keep from howling with pleasure. He was like someone possessed – powerfully dominating my hips, one hand clasped around my waist, the fingers biting into the skin as the other clasped down onto my shoulder the same way.

With every intention to meet the force of his need, I tried to rock my hips against his. Honestly, though… he was so incredibly fierce, controlling such a fast tempo, that I could barely keep up.

Instead, I allowed him to dominate me, continuously crashing against my hips with jaw-dropping intensity.

"Goddammit, Lex, that's so…"

"Am I hurting you?" He asked, pausing in mid-stroke. "I'm not hurting you, am I?"

The tenderness made my heart sing just a little, but I instead flashed him another sexy little look. "No, not at all… it feels so good, beneath your touch…"

"Good," he murmured hungrily, his eyes closing as he leaned his face back again. He gave me another powerful thrust, then continued: "That's what I like to hear."

He slipped back into powerfully fucking me, and I groaned with unending fulfillment.

"Oh Lex, you're so hot when you fuck me like that... I love feeling your hot, throbbing cock inside my wet pussy..."

He growled with contentment, picking up the speed just a touch. Obviously, he really did like what he was hearing...

"Please come for me, Lex. Come inside me. You know how badly I want it..."

His rippling arms tightened, and his fingers pressed ever harder into my skin. I almost yelped with pain, but soothed it to an excited, passionate squeal. The last thing I wanted to do was make him stop, and knowing how carefully he monitored my pleasure, willing to stop fucking me on a dime...

"Please give it all to me, Lex... every last drop inside you. I need it... I crave it..."

That seemed to do the trick.

His movements grew erratic, uncontrollable. Lex lost his grip on himself, rocking his hips against mine over and over, his heavy balls slapping against my skin as he visibly prepared for his own, stunning climax...

But his cock was pressing against my center so perfectly, and I *loved* being fucked in this position...

It was inevitable that I was about to come, myself. I steeled myself, shifting my weight against the headboard as I clenched up. Finally, the building tension shoved me off the precipice, leaving my gasping body moaning with complete orgasmic pleasure as I came hard against his hips, over and over.

As I burst through the multiple climaxes, Lex finally seized up, his limbs locking as he buried his rock-hard erection as hard into my slickened chasm as it would go. He let loose a roar, and I felt rope after rope of his thick, hot seed spurt into my body, surging deep inside.

After we came together, we collapsed down to the bedding and sheets, fulfilled and brought to the brink of satisfaction.

I nestled up against him as he rolled onto his back, completely spent from the consummation of our love. I felt his heart beating powerfully beneath his ribcage as my head slipped into place, and his arm wrapped around me.

"You mean the world to me," I heard him whisper as the throes of sleep came for me. All I could do was nod, quietly murmuring my agreement.

"I love you," I whispered.

"I love you too, Riley."

I felt safe.

I felt secure.

And I felt like the world was truly ours.

Epilogue

Riley

Six Months Later

As far as proposals go, dragging Gloria Van Lark into court was a pretty damned good way to get me to agree.

She had been true to her word, going to extreme lengths to sabotage my career. Gallery after gallery pulled my work. Lex kept me levelheaded through all of this. We were just gathering the evidence we needed.

The case was still tied up in court, but the world-renowned curator had lost a tremendous amount of influence in the art community, and her reputation was irreversibly tarnished as the truth of her escapades came out. Even if her lawyers were able to wheedle her out of any of the charges against her, despite her admissions, Gloria Van Lark would never enjoy even half the power she'd previously wielded.

And things were turning around quickly for my work... As it just so turned out... the *Spinnoc* museum was owned by an art collective known as the *Reinholdt Group*. The founder, Charles

Reinholdt, had dedicated his life and his great fortune to preserving priceless art across the world for many decades. With Gloria out of the way, the Reinholdt Group reached out to me directly.

My work made it to the *Spinnoc* after all…

Lex helped pulled a few strings and landed me a functional visa so we'd have time to set up a proper wedding. It beat getting hitched in Vegas…

My friends had taken my move overseas better than I could have expected… Connor and Reiko started dating not long after I left, and the two of them still come visit every once in a while.

They make a cute couple. Independent, working hard on their businesses together…

Connor even has a second location in the works.

On the day that Gloria Van Lark was marched into court, Lex proposed to me in front of the courthouse with one of the most beautiful rings I had ever seen. I couldn't possibly say no to such a stunning declaration, and I agreed on the spot – under the condition that we take the engagement slow, and truly come to learn each other.

He didn't see a problem with that... But he seemed to want to do most of his *learning* in the bedroom.

I didn't see a problem with *that* either...

And Lex?

Lex Lambert is still the same smug, confident, *world-class* football player that he was before. He still leads the English National team, although the team manager saw to it that a *certain* backstabbing rival was dishonorably removed from the team.

Maybe his face wasn't on a cereal box, but even that was only a matter of time. The sponsorship would be coming up again soon, and this time, Lex was the odds-on favorite.

Not that he cares. There are two things Lex is 100% invested in, me, and football. Well, I should say *us*, because after we talked it over... he decided to reverse the vasectomy.

We're going to try for a baby.

I'm out of my mind happy, and Lex is completely confident that this is going to be the year that England finally earns back its glory and retakes the World Cup…

And when he does…

I'll be in the stands, cheering him on, with my brand-new wedding ring glistening in the sun. I might even have our beautiful baby in my womb, ready to meet the world. I'll watch him lead his team towards victory as a beloved national icon and the most capable, loving man I've ever met.

I like the sound of that.

Maybe I'll paint that, too.